I'll tell the story,
even if no one is listening.

Originally published as *Dukkerne* by Forlaget
Basilisk, Copenhagen

This English translation first published in the
United Kingdom by Lolli Editions in 2021

The Dolls is No. 7 in the series New
Scandinavian Literature

Graphic design by Laura Silke
Cover illustration by Phil Goss
This book is set in Source Serif Pro
Printed and bound by TJ Books,
United Kingdom, 2021

This publication was made possible through the
generous support of the Jan Michalski Foundation,
the Danish Arts Foundation, and Konsul George
Jorck & Hustru Emma Jorck's Fond

The author would like to thank Sofie, Theresa,
Peter, Gustav, Jennifer, Denise, and not least Sophia.

A CIP catalogue record for this book is available
from the British Library

ISBN 9781999992842

Lolli Editions
132 Defoe House, Barbican
London EC2Y 8ND
United Kingdom
lollieditions.com

THE DOLLS

Translated from the Danish
by Jennifer Russell

URSULA SCAVENIUS

The Dolls

I sit at the table listening to the violin music that has started playing in the forest. I don't budge. Our house is just ten metres from the Centre. Here we are again, sitting around the table, nodding. Mother, Father and me. Like we do every evening. In our town something is often on fire; a car, a house, a bin.

We always agree. We agree that mince doesn't taste good, but that salt pork does. It's practically impossible to sleep at night with that violin music, says Father, and I repeat what he says. My sister Ella, who sits in the cellar, sings so loudly we can hear her through the floor. Then she starts to dance, and Mother lifts the trapdoor. Come upstairs now, it's dinnertime, she yells, but Ella only replies: No.

It's as if those violins are inside my head, says Father and passes Mother the saltshaker. Mother sprinkles salt on her food and stares out the window. The sound of violins from the forest grows louder. When chicken bones scrape against your teeth, it screeches in your ears. The violin bows gnaw at the strings the same way we gnaw at chicken bones. Violins, we keep calling them, but really it sounds like something else. Like chicken bones scraping against teeth.

Now the sound is softer. I crane towards the window to listen. The other day, our neighbour Kurt complained about the new refugees at the Centre disrupting the peace. All he wants is to go about his business, he says. Enjoy his evening coffee or a relaxing morning beer on his front lawn.

Here we are again, Mother, Father and me, listening to the music. Father puts his hands over his ears. I say that the chicken boiling in the pot on the stove all day is foul. Why, we'll switch to mince then, says Mother. That's enough mince talk, says Father. He puts down the drumstick on his plate and returns to the subject of the people across the street. The people at the Centre. We've got plans, Kurt and I, says Father, and I nod, tapping my feet against the floor to a steady beat. Stop that, says Mother.

That music has a certain, shall we say, violence to it, says Father. Here we are with empty plates, staring out at the children at the Centre. Mother nods, and Father starts to tap his spoon against his plate so that it sounds like a melody, like *Frère Jacques*. Would you stop, please? You're always playing that, says Mother. You know I love this song, says Father and sneezes. As a child I learned to sing songs from a songbook. Father nods: It brings people together. He hums. He has never looked happier. I hand him a spoon bigger than the one in his hand and he starts tapping my metal shin. It's rusty. Then Mother and Father stand up and clear the table.

Later on, Father tears a page from our calendar on the table. He writes on the back: *If anything ever happens, Agnes, just call Kurt.* He hands me the note. *He'll always be there to help you, Agnes,* he writes on another note. Mother holds her hand to her mouth. But Kurt is sick, she mutters into her palm. I hear her, but I don't think Father does. Mother gives Father a single hard whack across the back of his hand with the spoon.

I sit by the windowsill and listen to the music. I don't budge. Mother and Father are slumped across the table, sleeping.

A brown noctuid is sitting in a corner of the ceiling where mould has started to grow. It looks like a tiny cloak with two eyes, a crippled little creature quivering on the green patch of ceiling. It's been there for a week now, just like the magpie in the tree outside the window. I want to reach my hands up towards the noctuid, stretch out my fingers so far that a jolt of pain shoots through my chest.

While I wait for Mother and Father to go to bed, I wonder whether anything might happen between the noctuid and me, whether it will come any closer. I wait. Father and Mother get up at the same time. They walk to the bedroom in step. That pleases them. In perfect unison they give their duvets a few hard shakes and then they lie down and groan in their sleep.

I sit in the kitchen in my pyjamas listening to the music. In my head, everything is loud and white. The dark garden is dimly lit by a whitish fog. I lean over the stove and sniff the leftovers, then I curl over and hook my arms beneath my knees, taking up as little space as possible. Afterwards I roll my wheelchair back to the window and look down at the playground across from our house.

I listen. Some of the older children from school are still running about laughing on the playground, which is right next to the Centre. They don't like me. I go mad if I watch them for too long, but I can't help myself. One day I'll sneak over to Kurt's and borrow the camouflage face paint he keeps in his closet and blacken my face. I loathe my yellow hair and white skin. I refuse to look at myself in the mirror anymore, my eyes that shine. They look deranged, and that's why I've hung a dress over my mirror.

Mother coughs hoarsely in her bed. I have a splitting headache. How startled the birds would be if I were suddenly to jump out of the window into the fog. Perhaps I'd land at the bottom of the well where the little children once lay.

I'll never forget them; the little bodies Ella and I saw in the well last year. It was spring. In the May twilight, the bodies were practically indistinguishable from the murk of the well. And yet you could just make out the outline of three children. My sister had brought me outside to look into the well. Three little children with their arms around each other, bundled up in thick jumpers and nestled among blankets and pillows. As we peered down at the children, we heard Father's car come to a screeching halt in the driveway. He had come home later than usual that day.

Ella ran inside and sat down in the windowsill, and I chased after her. We wrapped ourselves in the blankets and waited. Father walked in and dropped a couple of sacks in front of us. Bald dolls and black hair came tumbling out. He asked us to bleach the hair and glue it to the dolls' heads. He planned to start a home production. At the Machine they only manufacture fake hair, he said, but this hair is real, it comes from India. If we dye it blonde, all the newly arrived refugee children will queue up to buy the dolls so they can be like the children whose families have always lived here. I think of that day often, because it was also the day Ella went into the cellar. Shortly after that, my leg went lame and I got the metal shin.

Each of you gets a few sacks, Father said, sitting atop the kitchen table to watch as we examined the contents of the sacks: black hair, bleach, needles, thread. We didn't play with the dolls. We were too old for that. You know what to do, Father said. We thanked him. My hands itched. I wanted to show him what I was good for.

I sat down on the floor with a doll in my hands and stared at it. Then I opened the bag of hair and began by washing it in the sink. Once I had mixed the bleach, I could start coating the hair with it. I made sure to coat all the black hairs evenly while Father looked on. Afterwards, he handed me a bag of healthy sweets. Now the blonde hair just needed to dry, then I could sew it onto the dolls' heads.

That was how Ella and I passed our final hours together before she went into the cellar. Before she went down there, we watched the grey ashes drifting onto the leaves in the garden, too. Ella hurled her doll at the wall and it landed bald-headed at her feet. You disgust me! Stop looking at me! she screamed. But Father and I looked at her all the same. Eventually she opened her own bag of hair. Then she stopped dead. I was best at working for Father.

The evening she went into the cellar, Ella told me that the grey flakes that drift onto the flowers came from children's burnt hair and fingernails.

I stopped dead when she told me that. We were in our bedroom, and I was staring at a doll. The glue on the doll's scalp had bubbles, and inside one of the bubbles was a pink star. I recognised that star. The doll had been in our house once before. It had lain in my lap, and it was me who had stuck that pink star into the tiny cavity on its head. It was still there, and I scraped it out with my nail.

The star had felt smooth against my fingertips, and I saved it in my pocket. Now I search my pocket for the little star, but it's gone. Ella has been in the cellar since May 20th. The day we were given the dolls to work on she went down into the cellar. She had growing pains and fell in love with that cellar.

Often we beg her to come back up, but she says: No, I like it down here. She says she's the tallest girl in town, and she's retreated to the cellar's darkness to keep out of the light so she won't grow any taller. She'll certainly also avoid infection and boils if she stays in the cellar, or *the room of lies*, as we used to call it.

A long time has passed since Ella went down there, and now I'm the only child sitting around the table. I listen to the music, which is distant and faint. So faint I have to be completely still and stop chewing to hear it. But it's there. I'd like to lose myself in the sound, but now someone knocks at the door, softly and firmly at the same time. I don't open, just carry on listening to the music outside. It sounds as though someone is practicing an instrument and has grown bored with it. I still sit here, listening.

Mother and Father come into the kitchen with Kurt between them. Mother hurries over to the sideboard and pulls out a bottle of vodka. Here! she says and casts down her eyes. Kurt places a 500-kroner note on the table. He glances over at the trapdoor to the cellar. Don't worry, he says. They're going to ban those violins soon. Then maybe Ella will come back up.

Shhh, says Mother. We don't even know whether it's violins. Mother speaks standing up while the rest of us sit. Then she sits down, and it seems to me she's expecting an answer. Kurt gets up and is about to take the vodka bottle from the table, but I roll over and swipe the bottle before he gets hold of it. In a split second Kurt goes from looking like a mad dog to the sick, scruffy old man he is. He's irritated now. What will he look like when he's dead, I wonder. Yellowish, maybe, or perhaps more white and green? I toss the bottle into the bin.

Well, time for bed then! Mother announces. She has yellow crosses in her eyes. Kurt responds by walking off but doesn't make it any further than the sofa, then he passes out.

The music outside has grown louder, and we listen together while we look at our drunken guest slumped on the sofa. Perhaps Mother and Father have also noticed the peculiar coincidence of the music and Kurt's snores. Should I help carry him out? I ask, without budging. Impossible. He'll let himself out when he wakes up, says Mother and stands up.

Don't forget to say goodnight to *her* too, she whispers, leaning over the trapdoor in the floor. Mother says goodnight to Ella, and Father does the same. I'm glad we don't have boils, and that Ella doesn't either. Down below, Ella hums along to the music. Unlike me, she can carry a tune. Father closes his eyes, clasps my hands and whispers: You're much too skinny, and you look like a boy. You don't have growing pains, do you?

We sit in the kitchen, Mother, Father and me, right above the trapdoor that leads to the cellar where Ella is lounging about, putting on makeup. She's beautiful, like Cleopatra, only taller. She often paints little purple stars on her nails, but today they're black with gold glitter. I've seen it through the little pipe we've stuck through a hole in the floor that's always been there. Most of the things the two of us had in our bedroom have been moved down to the cellar now. She's hung all our sheet music up on the walls.

As we listen to the violin music coming from the forest, Mother, Father and me, Ella sticks her hands up through the half-open trapdoor. She scrapes her nails across the floorboards. You'll ruin your nails doing that, says Mother, stroking the backs of Ella's hands, but Ella goes on scratching. It makes a crackling sound. We watch her hands. Sooner or later she'll surely retract them, I think, but she doesn't stop.

They could use a trim, whispers Mother. Let's cut them. I wheel over to search for the nail scissors in the kitchen drawer and can think of nothing but my sister's fingernails. Ella continues clawing at the floor while I rummage through the drawers. They're full of identical things; lighters, little torches, matches, clothespins, but no nail scissors.

Ella scrapes a particularly sharp nail across the floor, and I'm reminded of her hair, which never gets cut anymore, since she has no scissors of any kind in the cellar. Her too-long hair makes her look so skinny through the pipe in the floor. Her whole body has become long and scrawny.

Our cabinets are stuffed with identical goods Father has bought at the supermarket. He always gets ten of each thing on offer; ten jars of instant coffee in case the day comes when we can no longer leave the house. Ten packs of crispbread, and honey, one jar after the other, as well as butter, cheese, rye bread and potatoes in the fridge, but no nail scissors.

I wheel back to Mother and Father. They've found the nail scissors and are already busy cutting Ella's nails. Her hands lay limply across the floor like dead mouse tails. There's a tenderness to the way Mother and Father cut her nails, gently cradling Ella's slender fingers in their hands. They work together, and when they're done, they blow on Ella's nails and kiss her fingers one by one.

All of a sudden Ella yanks back her hands. The nail scissors fall from Mother's grasp. Mother and Father stop dead. For a while they just sit there, unmoving. Then, slowly, Mother reaches for the nail scissors, but I tickle her under her arms so she drops them. I slip them carefully into my pocket in case I should need them again.

The violins screech outside. I grind my teeth. Now it's the roots of my teeth that screech. I look through the window in my binoculars and see Kurt in the cemetery. He has his bucket with him and is washing the gravestone. Every day he goes to the cemetery with a mop and scrubs the gravestone until the name on it gleams. When he swings the mop across his shoulder, water drips down his back, but he doesn't notice. One time, on a Saturday, Kurt went out and buried his cigarette butts on his wife's grave.

It's getting to be winter. The sleet has softened the ground, and I can see the cigarette butts protruding from the soil. The moisture must have drawn up the cigarettes from the depths. Now everyone can see that it was true, the thing about the cigarettes on the grave.

We bury our memories of Hungary with her, and all the lies too, Kurt told Father the day they buried his wife. I remember her clearly, his Hungarian wife. Kurt uses washing powder for everything; for washing the dishes, washing himself, washing the gravestone. Through my binoculars I can see the gravestone up close. The dirt is sprinkled with lumps of washing powder. I can practically hear the stone weeping when Kurt washes it. People say his wife isn't even in the grave anymore. She's in a chamber pot beneath Kurt's bed, they say.

Two or three violins are screeching in the forest somewhere. I'm still sitting by the window. I fold a white piece of paper and write down the names of all the languages I don't speak. I put an X next to the ones I want to learn, and an X next to one that I'm afraid of, and next to one that others are afraid of. What I want most of all is to go to the beach and dangle my legs from the pier like I did a few years ago, back when I could cycle there.

I want to get out of here. Today.

The suitcase is out. When I board the bus I'll count to a thousand, and then I'll get off no matter where I am and that's where I'll spend the night! Something needs to happen. I pull a poncho over my head, covering my body as much as possible.

The door swings open. Kurt strolls into the kitchen. He extends his hand and says: My, you're looking fancy, aren't you! I look like his youngest son, he tells me, whose face is ghostly pale. He looks like he's got HIV, he sneers. There's not much ruddy-cheeked Hungarian over my son, I'm afraid! It killed his mother, him looking like that, says Kurt. People thought we had a sick son.

I don't reply to the part about his wife, because all I remember is how she would often fall into the roadside ditches when she came walking along with her shopping bag full of vodka bottles. Eventually she was hit by a bus when she was out buying vodka for Kurt, as she used to say.

Now Kurt sets a clinking bag on the floor and sits down to drink while he reads the newspaper. He opens another bottle of vodka, but then he pours the contents into the sink, rinses after and yells: No more drinking!

The music begins on the stroke of four. This time the violins sound plaintive and jarring, but Kurt doesn't threaten to smash the instruments like he usually does. But I can tell by the quivering bags under his eyes that the music is putting him in a bad mood.

Kurt stares into space. You could probably kill him if you played that music long enough, I think. Like when I think of the fingernail tree Ella and I made for Christmas when we were little. It always unsettles me to think of that tree. All through December we worked on the fingernail tree downstairs in the room of lies. It was made of two branches glued together with our fingernail clippings constituting the leaves. First we stuck on short nails, and afterwards we hung the longer nail clippings on the tree as fingernail Christmas decorations. It looked ominous, that tree.

Kurt never saw the fingernail tree, but he looks like someone who's thinking about it. Maybe that would do him off, seeing that tree. Like the sound of the music. I hold my hands over my ears to make it all go away. Kurt turns on the TV and grimly watches the tall, thin-haired people staring back out at us from the screen.

I lean out of the window and see Kurt plodding around in the cemetery. Light pierces through the rain when a bus drives past. A violin resounds in the forest. The sight of the pouring autumn rain rushing into the gutter makes my throat tickle. I want to lie down on the pavement in the rain or go walking past all the many empty houses. Stretch out my sore feet in my shoes, but of course I can't.

The violins grate outside. Now there's just a single violin; an unhurried bow stroke that sounds like a song sung deep down in the throat. The sound comes from somewhere among the trees, maybe even further away. The wind carries the music into the house. Perhaps it comes all the way from the beach. I can't tell. It's drizzling against the windowpane. I look up at the ceiling, like so often before.

Beneath the floor is Ella. Not a sound can be heard from down there. My voice is hollow in our old kitchen when I say her name. It sounds a little scratchy, like the violin strings. I look up at the ceiling and see the light bulb swinging back and forth.

On the window are two noctuids, and I open it to let them out. Fresh air streams across my face as I look out at the garden. The noctuids land in a puddle and flail about. A few more noctuids fly in through the window. They flutter about my ears, but they make less noise than the ones in the puddle. Over by the closet is another little swarm. Those are different, though. They're clothes moths. They come from somewhere on the top shelf where we keep the oatmeal. They look like the noctuids outside, only smaller. Father says they come from the Egyptian silk in Mother's wardrobe.

Now I stare at the cows on the hill behind the Centre. Study their tails through the binoculars. And I look at the autumn sky, which is slowly devouring the landscape, like a wave washing ashore. The houses look like stocky, big-eyed beasts, shrivelled up like piles of black seaweed on the beach. At five o'clock the sun sets somewhere beyond the rooftops, quick as a coin slipped into a piggy bank.

In the pasture behind the cemetery, no more than 15 or 20 metres away, stand the horses, dozing. A pine beside the house sways slightly in time with the music. The music stops. I wonder what Ella is up to downstairs? I stay close by and keep an eye on the trapdoor to make sure she's all right, but at the moment she hardly says anything at all, not even thank you.

Ella asked me to fetch an old rug, and then she told me: As soon as I've climbed down into the cellar, I want you to cover the trapdoor with the rug so no one will think of the entrance anymore. Then maybe they'll forget me, because that's what I want them to do. Mother and Father say that I've lied to everyone, and it's true. What I said at school about the children in our well was a lie. I told everyone that the grown-ups pulled out the children's teeth. I shouldn't have said that. Lately I've been getting thinner and taller each day, she said, and it's because I lied. Now I can't see my face in the mirror anymore, I've outgrown it. So I'm going to hide away until I stop lying and stop growing.

But before that, Ella had told me about the tortured children in the well. In the days leading up to her descent into the cellar, she couldn't stop talking about the children who lived at the Centre and had their teeth pulled out in our well one May night last year. She had looked straight through me as though in a trance as she told me over and over again how the grown-ups had deliberately burned the children's hair and thrown them into *our* well. At the end, she had whispered: Our parents were there, too.

Ella didn't want me to cheer her up before she went down there. Late that evening, she had grabbed a women's magazine, put on reading glasses and asked me to forget her for a few hours. Just for that night. Forget she was going into the cellar. I promised I would and took a long look at her skinny body in bed, her newly dyed hair, her blue-green eyes, her long, slender fingers gripping the magazine. She took up very little space in the bed, like a long straight line, and I whispered: Can I say something? It isn't very pleasant down there in the cellar. Pleasant, she scoffed. Who cares!

We weren't accustomed to loud sounds before the music started, but tonight it's blaring from the bog again. And it doesn't sound like violins, but like loud voices relentlessly roaring through enormous pipes. Rumour has it someone has found a barn full of violins, black and square. The people who talk on the TV say that the violins ought to be burned. That we must do whatever it takes to find those who break the laws and punish them so our citizens are kept safe.

A noctuid in the corner of the ceiling has grown bigger overnight. It's too big for me to enjoy looking at for very long anymore. Only now has its vile body become properly visible. I imagine it inside my mouth and it makes my stomach turn. The noctuid is the size of a kitten. It has spotted wings as heavy as bath towels that flap about from ceiling to floor and wall to wall. I slide down to the floor, hiding my face and arching my back.

The noctuid buzzes about like a bumblebee, and I feel it graze my skin as it zips past, testing out its wings to see how far they'll reach. It lands on my hair, but luckily it can't get through to my scalp. My hair is a fortress with no openings, I realise triumphantly. I press my face against the floorboards and hear the noctuid humming above me. It seems to have got the knack of flying and is soaring about the room as though that's all it's ever done.

I flip onto my back and try to fall asleep. The noctuid has returned to its spot in the corner of the ceiling. It looks withered, like a threadbare rug. I snap a picture of it with my phone. In the picture, it looks like a fossil.

After the click of the camera, it's silent. Then I hear a rustle from the trapdoor. It's Ella, poking up a message for me. Hastily I delete the picture of the noctuid. Why is she suddenly sending up letters? She pushes it up through the pipe in the floor. A note with her handwriting.

Dear Agnes, will you wrap up a boiled egg and drop it through the hole? That's plenty of food for me today.

Nothing has changed in this town since I was born, apart from the shops closing down. Now the sound of the music makes the walls of the house vibrate. I'm prepared to take off with the first person who walks through the door carrying a black instrument resembling a violin and says: Burn it if you like, but that girl is coming with me.

I'm not certain that it's violins or guitars or mandolins they're playing, because the instruments sound more like somebody beating an oil drum or sobbing from their belly. Father hollers for them to turn that music off right now!

The flies are sluggish, dropping to the floor in big piles. It's late now. The flies come buzzing up from the cellar through the pipe we exchange letters through. I listen to the whir of their tired wings in the corner of the windowsill, listen to them buzz as they wriggle about on top of each other before they die. I glance up at the noctuid, which no longer seems so big. It doesn't make any noise when it stirs in its corner. Tonight it appears to have closed itself off, silent as the people at the Centre across the street, where all the windows are dark. This is what it's come to; complete silence apart from the buzzing of dying flies.

More flies keep emerging from the cellar, attracted by the smell of the others' corpses. I send a boiled egg wrapped in parchment paper down the pipe to Ella. Ella sings for a little while. Then she falls quiet, as though she's listening to me, or to the flies. Suddenly the parchment paper pops back up through the pipe, now greasy.

I catch a glimpse of her through the pipe in the floor. Her long hair falls across her red-and-white striped shirt. She's got an old black computer down there. Her fingers rest on the keyboard but she never writes anything. I look for her through the pipe, but the chair is empty and the desk is cleared. I call for her, and her reply is loud, as though she were standing right behind me: What is it now? Just to say something, I whisper: Aren't the flies annoying? But there's no reply.

I whisper: You deserve a mosquito net. Peering through the pipe, I spot the little microwave next to Ella's bed. The lights are on down there. I sniff at the air rising from below; it's fishcakes. She's stopped eating red meat. She stands up from the bed and flatly declares: I don't eat fishcakes anymore, either. It does smell good, though, I whisper, but she just sighs.

There are too many flies. They get caught in my hair, she complains. I wouldn't worry about those flies if I were you, I hear Father yell from the living room, after all, they eat the spiders. No, Ella hisses from below, it's the other way around – the spiders eat the flies. Everyone knows that, Father! Mother laughs at them in the living room, and everything goes quiet. Ella doesn't shout sorry, nor does she accuse me. I wait to hear whether she'll say anything else. Then we quietly talk about homework, me in the incipient darkness of the kitchen, her in the shadows down below, in the steam of the fishcakes in the microwave. The smell drifts up through the pipe.

Here I am, peering down into the cellar at Ella. I don't ask her any questions, but pass down a few folded sheets of paper so she can do her homework. Father comes into the kitchen and cuts off a slice of a cutlet. We can't have her losing any more weight, he says and hunches over the pipe in the floor to look for Ella.

He calls for her: May we see you? How was your day? Not a word from below, no complaints. Then we swap places and I put my eye to the pipe. But she's nowhere in sight. Not so much as a pale shoulder or a foot. Do you want meat or fishcakes, Ella? yells Mother. You must remember to eat.

Father's breath smells rancid of old coffee. I still can't see Ella through the pipe, but there are plenty of flies. All those flies, they irritate her, I think. Maybe she's sleeping. I hear her toss and turn in her bed. The meat fumes make me nauseous. I lean over one last time to look through the pipe.

There she is. She comes slinking out of the shadows into the little circle of light from the hole above and smiles up at me. Then she lies down and sprawls out on the floor in her red jumper and red lipstick.

I long to tell lies with Ella again, but I can't think of anything to lie about. It's early in the morning. I hear Ella whisper something to me beneath the trapdoor. I put my ear to the pipe and listen. I never want to come back up, she whispers. Just give me a few books to read and a couple vegetables.

A violin screeches out in the forest somewhere. I cut a few slices of courgette and drop the thin rounds through the pipe in the trapdoor. Then I look out the window. Another violin starts to shriek somewhere out there, and I squeeze my eyes shut.

Yet another violin. My breath grows heavier, and I'm only half-listening. Then the music starts up in earnest. Ella hums along, the morning is dim, and I know she thinks no one can hear her. She hums and coughs, and I cough, and she hums. The music grows fainter, as though the musicians have strayed further from the road.

I put on my blue wool socks. They go up to my thighs and match my jumper. I drop to the floor and land on my hard metal shin. Then I pull myself back up into my wheelchair using the stove for support, taking a peek into the pot to see if there's more porridge. Mother and Father are still asleep. I woke up first, but I can hear Ella moving about in the cellar. I think she's wearing high heels, and that she's dancing. I hum. I hear her clacking her heels against the floor. Little pointy heels.

Ella strikes her heels against the floor again, and I open the window and sing. The music outside has grown louder. Someone is beating a drum, and it sounds like when we used to skip rope at school. The violins follow the rhythm. Some of the strings sound rusty, surely they'll snap soon, I think.

From the window I study the rose bed, which is sending a stench of rotten leaves all the way into the kitchen. I look at the perennials, which have turned into a thicket. All the things I usually look at. I lift my gaze, turn towards the forest and listen. Usually when they play their instruments, I stop to listen, but this time I try to block them out.

I see Father outside in the garden looking down at an old music box of ours that's been left in the grass. It tinkles and rasps, sputtering out an old children's song. He stares at the toy and picks it up, holding it to his ear. Then he sits down to smoke under the tree with the music box pinched between two fingers.

Now he walks light-footed to the workshop and returns with the toolbox, once shiny and silver, but now rusty. He stops dead on the lawn as though waiting for someone to give him permission to continue to the well. Then, shaking his head, he takes out a box of giant matches from the right side of the toolbox. He strikes the one match after the next and tosses them into the well. The flies won't be bothering you anymore! We'll smoke them out and stop them getting in through the well, he shouts in the direction of the house, probably hoping that Ella will hear him. There's a tunnel that runs between the well and our cellar. Maybe she can see the matches burning at the bottom of the well.

The smell of burnt fly flesh has drifted all the way from the well through the tunnel into the cellar, and now it rises through the pipe and into the kitchen. A swarm of flies comes wafting up from the well like a cloud. The rest of the giant matches have been left on the tree stump. Father strolls into the kitchen, humming. Ella yells: Thank you. The fire has freed her from the flies.

Wind blows through the open kitchen window straight

into my ears, and I scratch the sore openings with my fingernails. Ella sends a note up through the pipe, leaving a little sprinkling of flies on the floor. The music stops. Please, let Ella come back upstairs one day, I whisper. The note says:

Dear Agnes, I've found an aquarium. It leaks a bit. I've tied it to my foot.

I sit beneath the cooker hood in my wheelchair with a doll in my lap, pulling one hair after the next out of its scalp. I wind the black hairs around a cotton bud and stick the cotton bud into my ear so I can scratch the tenderest spot. It feels nice. An echo of the now-absent music continues to reverberate in my ears. There's no sound, yet it isn't entirely silent either. I can hear a whooshing sound. I think Ella must miss the music, because she's humming, trying to imitate the melody we've been hearing for weeks, and I smile. She said she tied her foot to the aquarium. I'll do that too, once I start to grow again. I chuckle to myself.

Here we are, the three of us, like so many times before, Mother, Father and me, sipping our tea. Ella sings, and Father says nothing. Not even when someone starts to practice the violin and it sounds as though it's their very first time. The sound is disorienting and raucous. Ella sings in the cellar.

Sing a different song! shouts Mother and lets out a long sigh, like when you leave the faucet running as you rummage through the fridge. That song of all songs, she adds. Father fishes out a pair of earplugs from his breast pocket. This way I won't be disturbed, he says, sticking the earplugs deep into his ears. Suddenly Mother gets up and goes outside.

I roll myself over to the window and see Mother stomping about in the vegetable patch, which has become unwieldy. The vegetables have all grown together; a carrot and a beet are tangled up, a courgette is intertwined with a cabbage head and the potatoes have fused with the Jerusalem artichokes.

Now even the vegetable patch has started telling lies, I think. To interfere would bring misfortune. Ella stops dancing while Mother goes on trampling the vegetables. Maybe she's listening to us from down below.

Mother stops moving in the vegetable patch. Violins seem to be playing, this time right nearby. It sounds like it's coming from Kurt's house, yells Ella from the cellar. Impossible, it was Kurt's wife who could play, says Father. He stands up too quickly and his earplugs fall out. He teeters. Then he falls over, hitting his forehead against the windowsill.

I roll over and grab hold of his arm to help him back up, but he's too heavy. The next moment he gets up on his own. What's the matter with you? he asks. I'm fine, he insists, and stalks off to put the kettle on.

He brushes lint from the carpet off his coat, glances in the mirror, takes a sip of coffee and paces around in figure eights. Shhh, he says, bending over to whisper into my ear. Why don't you watch Ella while we go to the meeting? It's about time we get this town under control! It will all get better once Mother and I move up the ranks at the Machine. He rubs his eyes.

We hear the violins screeching outside. Father points: Those instruments are forbidden!

The music surges in volume. The sound gets so loud it might damage our ears. It's a mournful march, playing so near that listening makes you fall apart. The music has never been this close, says Father. You would think it was

Kurt playing from his loo, says Mother, stepping inside to fetch her coat and purse. Father's legs shake and drool trickles from the corners of his mouth. He collapses again.

Mother lifts Father up off the floor and drags him to the sofa. She drapes a scarf over his face and says: I've got to go now. Father whimpers in his sleep beneath the scarf. Ella stomps around downstairs, humming. I hum along to the tune. I listen to Ella stomping and Father sleeping and the violins dwindling and then building in strength. Even when Mother is out of the house, there are still three of us, if you count Ella. There's only a floor between us.

I sit in the windowsill and look at the roses drooping on their stems, their heads soft as dumplings. I think back to when they first began putting entire human beings on the conveyor belt in the Machine, and after visiting I came home and threw up. I clearly remember how Father came home hauling an enormous gift to comfort me.

Birds perch on the branches with quivering wings. Their feathers drift onto the heavy dumplings below, the roses on their stems, but there's one bird among the thorns whose wings don't quiver. It flies over to our window and drills its beak right into the glass. It appears stuck, and I fear it might die. It must have eaten ashes like the others. Usually it's only the young that kill themselves after eating the ashes.

There was a special room inside the Machine where they would burn dead bodies, I remember. Afterwards, you could see smoke rise from the chimney.

My arms have grown so long and bony. Using my elbow I push the window open, and the window sash swings back. I grab hold of the scraggly bird and bring it inside, letting it drop onto the table. I flip it over, and on its belly is a splatter of red paint. Protruding from the paint are thick, stiff feathers which stick together, like sticky violin strings. I know that Egyptian scarabs are a sign of misfortune, but what about violin strings stuck to a paint splatter on the belly of a bird that has drilled its beak into a window?

I get things muddled up in my head. I see my reflection doubled in the window. You can get violin strings stuck in your throat, I tell myself out loud. Violins are used all over the world. That's what I've been told. There are all kinds of different violins. German violins. Arabic violins. Polish violins. Mongolian violins.

The bird reeks of paint. There's grey ash on the red splatter on its belly, and a shard of glass is lodged in its eye. I set it on the windowsill and nudge it. It flies off. Outwards, across the grass. And then lands, a bit clumsily, in a tree.

Kurt is on the playground outside with a rifle in his hands, watching me as I toss the bird out of the window. Does he see it fly up and land on a branch, too? It was Kurt who reported the fire the other day. A car stood in flames for a short while, but after the fire was extinguished the car glittered like gold. So far it's only cars, houses and bins that get set on fire. I watch Kurt stagger back and forth across the playground. He bats at the swing. He only has one eye that can see, the other is green and made of glass.

An impermeable fog is draped across the trees and the grass. Ashes come drifting down through the fog. Kurt leaves the playground, brushing the ash off his clothes before he disappears into his house. I drink the rest of my tea and set the cup in the sink. All at once my legs fall asleep, but I still feel a tickle beneath the soles of my feet. It's Ella, sending up another note through the pipe in the trapdoor.

Will you help get me a hotplate and a frying pan? We can arrange a day when you open up the trapdoor all the way. Until then, would you please fry the eggs and wrap them in parchment paper instead of boiling them? Boiled eggs make me sick. They go all purply-yellow. Anyway, time to practice French vocabulary.

The porch light switches on when Father walks through the garden. He disappears into the playhouse-sized dollhouse that Mother bought for our future little brother. The walls inside are patterned with what looks like millions of eyes swirled together. Little Brother is coming in eight months, but the dollhouse is big enough for Father to sit and smoke inside.

The night is white. The light from the lamp outside outlines the garden's contours. A night as white as the toppling statue of a dictator. The white hour. Father's white eyes. I see him through the kitchen window. I grab my binoculars to take a closer look. Father's silhouette. He's hunched over in the dollhouse with the newspaper and a torch. The fog is white. His face is white. I hold my breath.

Father is sitting in a child-sized armchair. He rolls his earplugs back and forth across the newspaper on the table. I try to smile at him, and he looks my way. That's what it feels like. Now it's just the two of us, Father and me. Me with my binoculars in the kitchen. Father in the dollhouse. I look at him through the window, and he looks back at me.

We listen to the music. His pupils are small. I feel ill at ease when his pupils are small. A jolt of pain shoots through my chest and elbow. His pupils shrink and the pain seems to shoot through him, too. His eyes narrow. I listen to the music. I lean out of the window like I often do and watch

Father as he crawls back out of the dollhouse. He walks over and stops in the glow of the porch light, regarding me through the open window. Why are you interfering? he asks. I'm not interfering, I say. I'm only sitting here to get some fresh air.

He hands me a little brown paper bag through the window. I open it. It smells of cake. On the front of the bag is a picture of a laughing Santa Claus. But Father, sugar makes me go mad, I whisper, trying to give back the bag. Remember when I ate cinnamon buns and they gave me wild ideas? Relax, Snow White, he says, pulling a gold filling out of the bag. It isn't cake. We're not idiots, are we? He pulls out another gold filling. No cake. Just teeth. In case it all goes wrong, he leans forwards and whispers as were he stroking my hair. My own private insurance, he says with a look of despair.

I have to do something about that look, do something quick, but I can't speak or think when it smells of cake, so I just close my eyes and pray that he'll leave. Where all the gold fillings come from he doesn't say. They gleam in his palm. Then he drops them back into the bag. They jingle. He stuffs the bag into his pocket and comes inside. He sits down beside me and offers to help me to bed. Mother is asleep. Father hums along to the tune of the violins in the forest and carries me up the stairs.

At the sink we wash our hands under the same jet of water. He hums a psalm, and outside the sky starts to rumble. Here comes the apocalypse, he says. I listen to the rumbling sky and the clattering of the bathroom window, which isn't properly shut. A storm is brewing. Father smells of ash.

I sit in the kitchen after a night of listening to the storm. The dolls lie on the floor in a little puddle of water that sparkles in the morning light. I slide myself out of the wheelchair and touch their pink skin. Some of them still have hair on their heads. Little tufts of blonde hair, glued on here and there. The rest of the bleached hair floats about in the puddle on the floor. Water from the garden is seeping in through a tiny gap between the wall and the floor.

Mother is gluing the blonde tufts of hair onto the bald heads of the remaining dolls and drying off of their cheeks. Not a word passes over her pursed lips. Her eyes shine like marbles. She watches as I catch a spider in a glass just as it's about to dart across the kitchen counter.

I catch a whiff of rotten apples every time a rose branch moves outside. It mingles with the smell of stables emanating from Mother's clothes. Mother sighs the way she does when she's disappointed in one of us.

I look at the blue bus parked in front of the Centre. It doesn't look like the other busses. I ask Mother about it. She's silent for a while, then she says: It's the bus that's always empty when it arrives and full when it leaves.

We keep staring at the bus as we listen for the music, but in vain. We listen and shake our heads. The music is missing, but none of us mention it, as though it were impossible to admit out loud. Father stands in the middle of the room and stares at me. All at once the violins start to play in the bog, and the sound gradually builds, like a radio being turned up. Why are they doing this? asks Father. Why are they doing this to us?

Several families from the Centre start to board the bus. I try to throw myself to the floor. I don't want to hear Father speaking ill of the violins.

The bus drives off. Now of all times I need the music!

I reach out to close the window. We'll get sick, says Father, and then we'll be the ones on the conveyor belt in the Machine. Yes, but better to die than become useless, says Mother and sits down at the table. She looks out at the road where Kurt is pulling along a wagon covered with a tarp. It's pouring rain. Water has started to seep up onto the floor from the cellar, too. Ella can't possibly be down there, I tell myself, but I don't dare roll over and check through the pipe. Mother just sits and stares with a wooden spoon in her hand.

Father looks at her. Then he yells: I've got it! We'll build a wall!

We'll build a wall. Father sings the words. Then we'll be rid of the music. He calls for Kurt, who comes running. What's all this racket? he asks. And Father shouts: We're building a wall to keep out the music. It isn't worth the trouble, Kurt laughs. The music seeps in everywhere. But at least you'll block the Centre from view. I'll help!

I hear a soft thud. Father parks a wheelbarrow on the lawn. The sun is setting, and it blinds me. For a moment everything in the garden goes white: the clouds, the trees, Father. Then the colours come back, bathing the garden in shades of pink. Father starts sawing down the old fence, and he doesn't notice me watching him as he saws and saws. The sound of the chainsaw goes on and on. I yell at Father and Kurt to turn it off, but they don't answer, and the noise continues, even after dark.

I hear various sounds from the garden. The wall is nearly finished. The planks from what used to be our fence are now piled up on the lawn next to the bricks, which shine, all smooth and beautiful. Father and Kurt spread mortar between each brick and stack them one after one. They push the wheelbarrow back and forth until I'm convinced the house is a ship that's rocking, and at that point I know I'm asleep.

I sit in my wheelchair as always. They've wheeled me outside and left me next to the buckets of mortar. We haven't said a word. Mother and I haven't spoken this morning. We sit in the garden looking at the mortar in the driveway and the rainwater rushing into the gutter. Neither of us attempts to speak with the few people left at the Centre on the other side of the new wall.

Everyone in the garden has whitewashed skin from the work with the plaster. A car speeds past. I watch it go and touch my skin. I roll over to the house and study my reflection in the window. My eyelashes are all white. My face is covered in a layer of white tinged with silver, just like Father's.

Mother hands me a pen and tells me what to write, for example: *It's forbidden to climb the wall. It's illegal to play instruments that have not been approved.*

We're going to hand out flyers.

Something smells burnt. Someone in the Centre is shouting and singing. Now the remaining foreigners are behind a wall. I won't be able to watch the children play anymore. Mother asks me to write: *People who approach the wall may be shot.*

We've got to stick together, she says.

The water mixes with the plaster in the wet grass.

I've started to believe there are people watching me from on top of the wall. If there were music it might help take my mind off it, but the music is no longer there.

Someone is watching me from up on the wall, I think again. I need the music to better see. Ella doesn't hum, she doesn't dance, she's silent and indifferent. Ella has forgotten us, and she's lied. She's so quiet I doubt she's even in the cellar anymore. Before, she used to dance and sing and hum along to the music, but now she's forgotten us, forgotten her roots. Sometimes I think she's left us for good. Not just temporarily, or to tease us, but forever.

It smells like rotten eggs when you put your face to the trapdoor. I really think she's been lying to me. That she's had me send down eggs to her for days without being there to eat them; that those eggs were just a diversion.

It downright reeks of eggs from the cellar. I try not to inhale the stench. I take the cap off of one of Ella's lipsticks and apply a thin layer across my lips.

Mother has gone so quiet. She's been this way ever since the wall was built and the Machine was expanded, enlarged and made mobile. She says nothing when Father and Kurt talk about how we've got to defend ourselves.

Mother was silent when the music disappeared too, and when Father told us that the workers at the Machine had ground up all the violins they could find in the forest. Mother only speaks when the violins play. Now a new sort of music has begun.

Father looks out the window. He removes one earplug to listen. I laugh to Mother: Father looks like a dead chicken still scrambling about. Father peers through the binoculars at the Centre's office. Inside sits the manager in the light of a lamp. She's got a lighter in her hand and is burning our flyers about the violin ban.

Father slips the binoculars back into his pocket. I help Mother get the tea ready. We set out teacups and arrange biscuits on a platter, and then we sit and have our tea. We hold hands like we always do while we look over at the Centre. We can't see what the manager looks like, only the top of her wavy-haired head.

There's a small orchestra and a conductor out on the field. The conductor sways slightly from side to side. I rummage through the drawers for earplugs. The conductor is wearing knee-high red boots. He bobs his head and makes the musicians follow his swaying. Tubas, trumpets. Each musician has their own shrill way of interpreting his movements.

The new, thunderous music is an interpretation of his red boots and long, dark-blue coat, his mother-of-pearl scarf, his lanky legs and long fingers. All the new musicians are tall and blonde. There's no stopping them. They go on playing, even when people yell 'Stop!' from their gardens.

They're practicing for a concert on Saturday, says Mother, let them be. She doesn't take her eyes off of the conductor's wriggling body. He's almost twice as tall as Father. More slender, younger.

I realise there's something about the look in Mother's eyes. Something has fallen out of her gaze, I think, like when a screw falls out of a clock so it no longer runs. Her pupils are like tunnels leading through her eyes to her brain. When she stares out at the conductor, she looks evil.

Father grew furious and stormed out when Mother told

him there would be no Little Brother after all. No one knows where he went. He doesn't have any Machine to go to, because he got fired. He doesn't have any Kurt to go to, because Kurt is working at the Machine. I never see Kurt at the cemetery anymore. Maybe Father is in the dollhouse? I haven't kept track, I can't bear to look for him.

Mother gets up. The look in her eyes is sinister and cold. She walks outside, picks up an axe off the ground and swings it against the wall. The axe lodges itself in as if it's growing out of the wall. Mother comes back inside. A wall with an axe in it is better than just a wall, she says.

The conductor on the field twists his knees rhythmically from side to side, and the orchestra's music goes from choppy and shrill to serene and fluid. I miss the old music we used to hear from the forest. This new music is evil, I think, like Father, who left, and Little Brother, who isn't coming, and Ella, who has abandoned us, and Mother, who has taken on an evil gaze. All of them, evil.

The conductor twitches. Maybe he'll be in charge of the town from now on, I think. The conductor sips from a bottle of water and wipes away the sweat under his arms, takes off his jumper and pulls a new, bigger jumper over his scrawny frame. Now I see his face. He's not the sort you see around here. His face is pear-shaped, and he has long, straight, whitish hair.

Early morning. Just 20 steps away from Kurt's house stand the old musicians. I hear them start to play again. It's the music we used to hear from the forest, for months; the violins. Chinaman music, as Kurt once called it. The two melodies play simultaneously; the old and the new intermingle. It's as though both groups have been practicing on their own and are now coming together. And someone is inside Kurt's house staring out at the musicians, someone in a big men's parka of blue canvas.

Later I get out the binoculars and peer into Kurt's living room. Kurt is sitting hunched over in the alcove where he sleeps, staring into space. The alcove towers up in the low-ceilinged farmhouse. He spits. A gob of slime lands beside the spittoon at his feet. He sticks one leg out of the alcove. Another gob of spit lands in the spittoon. He can't go running to the sink every time he needs to spit.

I watch in silence as he swings both legs over the side of the alcove. He climbs out, grasping someone's hand in his. A woman tumbles out of the alcove and lands on the floor, still asleep.

Kurt takes off his shirt and scratches his chest. Then he takes off his trousers too and stands there naked in front of the woman while he pours a glass of vodka. She drinks it, then coughs and squirms. It's my sister, Ella, in Kurt's house. Still lying on the floor, she wriggles out of the parka and hastily turns away.

Ella looked so scrawny in the parka. My vision goes cloudy. Kurt picks up Ella and carries her around. She tears herself free, puts on a jumper and kicks him to the ground, puts her foot on his big fat belly and smiles at me, or at least that's what it looks like, then sits down at the table to eat. Kurt gets back up and potters about, puts on his coat and leaves.

Kurt has left his house in Ella's hands.

Meanwhile, he's in the cemetery, drinking beer in a

folding chair on the grave. Ella walks over to the window and looks straight at me. I fix my eyes on her, as if with my stare I could keep her from disappearing.

Father walks through the door after having been out all night and goes straight to bed without his morning coffee.

From his place on his wife's grave, Kurt keeps an eye on the old musicians, the old music that has started to play again. He's the one who has always said: Those violins should be crushed or burned. Those violins should be banned. The fact that they've returned after all the times he's tried to get rid of them is a personal defeat.

Evening has come after a long, uneventful day. Ella roamed around in Kurt's house. Father slept. Kurt sat on the grave. Now it's nine o'clock, and Mother forgets all about our evening coffee. She stands next to me and looks to see what I'm looking at: Kurt, who has gained a small entourage in the cemetery. Someone from the group shouts into a megaphone: We need to find the musicians' camp. Where are they hiding? Kurt and his group abandon Kurt's wife's grave and head for the forest. We watch as the flickering torches gradually disappear among the trees, on the hunt for discarded illegal instruments and any old musicians still hanging about.

Ella could come home at any moment, I think. I don't want to read her escape as a sign that she's left us for good. Maybe she'll come home soon.

Birdsong. A light evening. I watch Mother drill a hole in the wall with an electric drill. That way we can keep an eye on the Centre, she said before grabbing the drill and going outside.

Father sits in the kitchen and stares at the guards who have taken their posts around the Centre. They don't want to overlook anyone, people say. Should an old musician come by, they'll catch him. Father keeps an eye on the guards. I suspect that Father is only sitting around staring to stay on the guards' good side, in the hopes that they won't come here and clear us away! But the people patrolling outside smile and wave at Father as though he were a retired commander.

Don't you want to go to bed?

Mother is standing in front me, asking. I wake up without actually having slept. No, thank you, I say. I'm waiting for Ella, but I don't tell Mother that. I don't mind sleeping here, I say, and Mother goes to bed.

It's a bit colder than the other nights, but lighter, and Father stays up half the night, staring grimly at the wall outside from his seat in the kitchen. I sit completely still in my wheelchair. The clouds have slipped off the sky. It's almost too beautiful. An ice-cold starry sky. A single lantern blinks in the distance. A guard sneezes. It sounds like a howl from the moon.

The bushes outside by the rubble shake in the wind. Should I get sterilised? I wonder as I roll my wheelchair around in the kitchen with the lights off. Ella doesn't appear even once in Kurt's window. Where is my sister?

Morning light. Mother is in the garden. She's wearing high heels and a blazer and wobbles slightly as she strides across the lawn. Then she yanks at the axe, which is still firmly lodged in the wall. It doesn't budge. She takes out a box of matches and tries to set fire to the wall. That doesn't work, either. It's raining. I can tell she's deliberating something. She makes up her mind and coolly marches past the window over to the car. Then she drives at full speed straight into the wall, which starts to teeter. She rams the car into it once more. A couple of children come running out of the Centre to watch as the wall comes toppling down.

Mother stays in the car with a smile on her lips. Kurt walks past with a basket of apples. He starts to roam about in the rubble. His hair is two different colours; there's grey in the blonde, the dye no longer hides it. He's hunting for something among the bricks. I look back and forth between Kurt and Mother in the car. But then I turn my gaze to the floor. There's a note from Ella beneath my feet. That means she's back in the cellar! She must have crawled in through the well. *Dear Agnes. Our fingernail tree has broken in half, and the dolls are rotting in their sacks. I don't know what to do about it, and I'm tired of it being my responsibility alone. I'm not even kidding. I'd like to try coffee now that I've turned 20. Would you please send down some of Mother's instant coffee? Someone has thrown an electric kettle through the cellar window. Was that you, Agnes? It was a while ago. It's full of limescale, but it works all right. From Ella.*

Father sits arrested at the kitchen table with a wilted rose in his hand. He smiles very slightly, but it's definitely a smile. Look what Mother gave me last night, he whispers, rubbing the rose across his eyes.

I put down the note from Ella I've been clutching to my chest and fetch the scissors from the drawer.

They feel cold in my hand. No one sees me cut off my hair. It's as though I'm invisible as I focus on the rustling of the pines until all other sounds fade away. I have just a single wish left: for Ella and me to become as small as the children Ella saw in the well, the children I too saw in the well one May night long ago. As small and as dark as they were before we were told to put blonde wigs on their heads, and before we took them to the Machine for assessment. Some made it, others were left behind in the well or burned.

I think about it all the time: Ella and I were told to put the dark-haired children on a conveyor belt in the Machine, back when it was still just a small stationary factory. Now it's expanded and turned mobile, which means it can go wherever it pleases. At the moment it's out in the fields.

We had to glue the blonde wigs onto their heads, and we were told to paint their skin yellowish-white and put blue contact lenses on their eyes. In the control room, we were meant to push the green button if we believed the children would be able to get jobs. It was up to us to determine their future.

And we chose to press the green button, Ella and I. We believed in them, and we watched as the children's bodies were carried off on the conveyor belt to the main office. One little body after the next in blonde wigs, wigs made of our old hair, all the hair we had collected year after year in big sacks in the cellar. Later, once we ran out, we bleached the new black Indian hair, which was cheap to buy.

What happens if we press the red button? I once asked Kurt's wife, who always guarded over that button. She knew better than anyone what could happen if you pressed it. The men who were drunk would come along and deliberately trip and hit the red button, causing the conveyor belt to go the wrong way. It was a big, round button made of red plastic. Not hard to see, not easy to forget.

All I had to do was press the button, and I always chose the green one, unless I got distracted, tricked by drunken Kurt. Stick to the green button, Kurt's wife told us when no one else could hear. But what about the red button? we kept asking. Stay away from it, she warned. But one time I did press the red button, the time Kurt tricked me.

I still remember it. I sit in the kitchen. The pile of red onions in Mother's ravaged vegetable patch looks like a row of those red buttons. I watch Father bow over the table and pound his head against it. I can't stand it. I want him to stop.

I wheel over and run my wheelchair into him. Father, I say, Father! I want to tell you something. Ella has been hiding at Kurt's! But now she's back in the cellar, she hasn't left us after all! Father sits down and lights a cigarette. He narrows his eyes at me and smiles: I've got to admit, Agnes, your imagination can certainly stop a person in their tracks – only for a moment, but nevertheless. Then, triumphantly, he smiles.

I sit on my own and look down through the opening into the cellar. It's become so quiet down there. Mother smashed the trapdoor to pieces all on her own! From up above, the cellar room looks like a cabin on a ship. It feels reassuring now that there's a hole leading straight to Ella. But she's vanished again. She would dance and sing down there, but now she's gone. My legs tingle for a moment, then I can't feel them at all.

Mother rests on the sofa below. I study the Persian carpet that adorns the floor. It's faded and worn from the water that has now flooded the cellar three times through the tunnel from the well. The floodings have dulled the carpet's red colours. We ought to burn it before it gets wet again, I think. Use a weed burner so we can see what's underneath. Maybe flowers have sprouted from the floor in the meantime. Or perhaps it's covered in yellow and black crosses. Yellow crosses or spider crosses?

The cellar walls have been painted pale green, I now realise. I hadn't noticed before. Apart from that, only the smell of mildew reveals that the cellar has been locked up for so long. I smile. I know Ella is down there somewhere, hiding from me. It means I can still look for her, or just keep on waiting, and one day we'll be able to work together, tell lies together, make fingernail trees together and I can ask her whether she'll get sterilised, too.

I feel like the music is coming from my throat, as if it's me screeching and not the violins in the forest. Mother pops her head out of the cellar and looks at Father and me, baffled. Then she climbs back up through the hole in the floor.

We sit and listen to the music, the three of us, like so many times before, Mother, Father and me, and the music creaks like icicles in frost, penetrating our soundproofed windows. Look who's playing out there, says Father without a trace of anger and points. Just outside the window is a tiny orchestra. They could be carted off by the police any moment. One musician has a drum made of goat's skin. Another, a little flute. Father laughs: It must be a Turkish quartet.

And we laugh, the three of us. Mother drops a slice of

apple into her lap. I take her hand and close my eyes. The musicians go on playing outside our window, amidst the rubble that's strewn across the lawn.

The musicians have left. Kurt comes into the kitchen with his gravestone mop slung across his shoulder. He rants about the mud at the cemetery and reports that there's no getting anywhere after dark due to the puddles. Why don't we take an evening walk and chase them away? he asks Father, nodding towards the Centre. Surely you're not backing down?

Kurt's eyes look like two incisions cut into an apple when he laughs that way. He stares at Father, and Father's smile is gone. Extinguished, like when you blow out a candle. Not slowly, like other people's smiles, but in an instant.

Kurt and Father disappear across the field to the Centre. Through the binoculars I see them trudging past the abandoned farm by the road, past the horses roaming silently in the paddock with their heads bowed. Mother and I go on dipping our biscuits in tea, and I can't help but look out for Father and Kurt.

Along the main road, there is light in the little lamp above the front door of some of the houses, but most are turned off, and in front of the peeling picket fences stand crooked *For Sale* signs. Father and Kurt grope their way towards the Centre. I'm still watching them through the binoculars. They stop at the sports hall at the far end of the Centre, which used to be a school. Kurt puts his palm against a tall wall. He examines the concrete and lights a cigarette with his lighter.

Father and Kurt peer through the windows of the Centre for a while. That's where I went to school, right there, where the children now play.

Father and Kurt empty a can of petrol through an open window in the sports hall, which is rumoured to be a dormitory for the children. A lighter flares. They throw giant matches through the window, too. The fire starts to flicker inside. The wall lights up, and shortly after it becomes a golden line of flames. Father and Kurt dart off to the right of the burning Centre and disappear around the corner.

It's late at night. We gaze out at the darkness and the blazing flames, Father, Mother and me, and Mother says: The neighbours have rolled down their blinds. It takes some nerve to simply lower the blinds when someone in town is screaming.

And Father replies: At least our windows are open. Yes, you're right, says Mother. At least our windows are open. We're not complete reactionaries.

Father drums his fingers on the table and hums a tune. Now Kurt and his entourage are stomping through town again, barging into houses with their bottles, cigarettes and heavy boots.

There are three of us around the table; three of us listening to the silence which is interrupted by screams from the burning Centre. There are two of us who watch Father stand up, put on his coat and mumble disjointed sentences about being fed up, about leaving everything behind. Mother throws herself at Father's feet to stop him from leaving. The sound of the screams outside mix with the sound of Mother begging Father to stay. Father collapses next to Mother on the floor.

Mother and Father lie on the ground clutching one another. I watch TV.

It's long past eight in the morning, but none of us are going out. I keep an eye on everything, and I get the feeling that I'm the only human here. The people inside the TV have wax faces, and they report that the Machine will be expanded further. Everything is going swimmingly in our village, says the balding newscaster.

Across the street, residents come pouring out of the burning Centre, struggling to bring their bags, bundles and suitcases with them.

The doorbell rings. Mother and Father creep across the floor towards the bedroom, but before they make it very far the door swings open. In the doorway is Kurt, dressed in a long fur coat with the buttons undone. Kurt in long johns under his coat. Kurt who never wears proper clothes, not even in winter.

He winks at us and laughs loudly, strolls inside and sits down at the kitchen table. Reaches for the coffee pot. Now he winks at me specifically and whispers: It's a shame you live right next to the Centre. Guess who they suspect burned the whole thing down?

And I see that his face is turning into wax too, just like the people on TV.

I stare at his congealed-looking skin. There's something odd about his legs, too. They're shaking. Then they stiffen. They want to interrogate me even though I'm sick as a dog, Kurt whispers, his eyes darting all around. Father reaches for the newspaper, shakes his head. I'll bet one of those pigs lit it on fire themselves so people would feel sorry for them, laughs Kurt. They're animals. Then, looking fearful, he whispers: But there is the matter of... He sticks out his tongue. It's swollen and covered in boils. Mother gives him an ice cube. Rub this on it, she says, that usually helps. No,

Kurt snarls and lets the ice cube drop to the floor. I'm fine.

His tongue protrudes over his lips a little. He has difficulty speaking. Someone drew crosses on the windows, notes Mother. So what? Kurt replies and flops onto the sofa.

Mother rubs Kurt's eyes with an ice cube, massaging the purply-red bags beneath them. Then she passes the ice cube to Father, who takes over the task of icing Kurt's skin. He rubs Kurt's tongue, and this time Kurt doesn't protest. He's asleep.

There's an artichoke leaf stuck in my throat and I'm trying not to listen. There's no way to prove whether the screams are real, someone on the radio says. The screaming and shouting seem human. There could be people being tortured right now. It sounds real, but these days anything could be propaganda.

Here we are again, the three of us, eating artichokes and listening. We chew our food meticulously while we listen to the screams from the other side of the toppled wall. Obviously, we can't just run out and help when we don't even know whether the screams are real. First we have to be sure that it's real people who are screaming, says Father, and we agree.

If it is real people, it's too late anyhow. Best we forget and start afresh, he says. We eat big, fresh artichokes and enormous string beans. Our plates are all green. The screams are softer now. It could sound like the end of a nightmare, right before you wake up.

We listen to the muted screams. We cut our artichokes with the blunt side of the knife and chew noisily, with no regard for manners. It sounds as if the screams are coming from inside our ears. The echo of something dreamed. Not something here in town.

I lean over and take Mother's hand. I look at Father's. He drums his fingers against the table out of sync with the screams, and I don't know what comes over me; I stuff his knuckles into my mouth and bite down, hard. He flings me away like a piece of seaweed on the beach and continues his out-of-sync drumming. Then he slumps in his chair. Mother pulls me onto her lap. We seem so big compared to Father's crumpled figure across the table.

We'll sit here until it's over, says Mother.

I hear children crying and grown-ups yelling. Mother's pupils gleam. They look yellow. I look out into the garden. The ashes dance like silver in the light.

We can't sleep when we listen to the reverberations that rise from the skip into which the shattered instruments were tossed. It's unsettling, the reverberation from the broken instruments. None of us can sleep when there's a violin string sticking out of the skip. So here we are again by the window, gathered around the kitchen table. Mother with her head in her arms and Father leaning back, his face turned up to the ceiling.

I stare at the violin string protruding from the skip, and at a shop sign that says *Closed.* I can clearly make out the writing on some newspapers flapping in the skip from which the last echoes of the broken violins ring out, and one of the scraps reads: *New extension of the Machine underway.*

I crush a pile of sleeping pills against my plate and sprinkle the powder onto the floor.

The muted screams continue behind the wall. There are three of us, Mother, Father and me. The sun gets bigger and turns red. Father says: We belong together. The sun becomes enormous up in the sky above the rubble, and I watch it grow from where I sit.

First the sun goes cold. Then it gets hot, colouring the whole garden red. Blinded, we chuckle to each other, and in the red light I feel Mother's hands, and my heart beating in my skin. My voice is an instrument played by a cheerful orchestra. The garden, the church, the wall and the clouds all resound in our laughter like a piano in the air.

Early this morning Kurt hobbled off on crutches towards the new Machine, which is now located where the Centre used to be. It has started to snow. It's snowing more than it has for the past 80 years, says Mother. And she says: You never know when it will get colder than ever, or when it will get hotter.

But the Machine goes on belching out toxic fumes no matter the weather, and the old grocer has run out of beer, vodka, lottery tickets and tinned mackerel. That's what Kurt shouts as he staggers past our windows and over to the Machine, trailed by several more townspeople. I watch them from the window in the kitchen. At our house we live off instant coffee and vitamin powder. We've been stocking up in advance, says Father. He has pinned an old medal to his shirt and an identical one beside Mother's neckline.

We watch Kurt position himself in front of the funnel beneath the Machine. He tries to catch the goods that fall out by mistake every once in a while. He pushes at the Machine, trying to make it teeter so more goods will fall. Nothing does. He's left empty-handed, and so are many others. People have run out of goods.

A storm has started to rage. The Machine, which has expanded yet again, rolls back and forth a little. Covering the road are big, beautiful snowdrifts, unlike anything we've ever seen before. The enormous Machine, which is now visible all the time from our kitchen, is covered by a thick, white blanket of snow. I see Kurt knocking on the Machine as if it were a silo-sized coffin. He nearly vanishes in the smoke from the Machine and the snow. Then there's a faint hum of the new music over on the field, and I cover my ears.

When I see Kurt in front of the big Machine shining so brightly in the snow, I wish he would just climb right in and disappear, as though into the mouth of an animal. The other townspeople have joined Kurt. They stretch their hands out towards the Machine, which starts to roll in the direction of the shivering masses. It's impossible to see who is inside the operator's cabin driving the Machine, but whoever it is, they take no notice of who the Machine hits on the snowy ground below.

Kurt is standing in a big snowdrift with his crutches. The Machine comes closer. Scrawny bodies leap to all sides like droplets from a showerhead, but Kurt stays put. He lifts the crutches and waves them about, pounds them against the Machine and gets run over.

Hasn't the Machine moved in on us since Kurt's death? Last time we checked, there was a street's distance between us and the Machine. Now it's right outside our windows, blocking the view.

Mother opens the window and I reach out to touch the Machine, and right then it rolls all the way up to the house. It's so close I can touch the side of it, its walls are smooth, and I can see inside the Engine Room, that's how close it is. I can see goods on the conveyors belts serenely gliding past, but no children.

We'd better enjoy ourselves, because my guess is we'll be gone by next week, too, says Mother.

The Machine has quietly moved so close it's now grazing our walls. Father crawls beneath the table with a doll in his lap, something I've never seen him do before. Absent-mindedly he cradles the doll, which is missing its eyes. He stares into her empty eye sockets and says: It was nice back when dolls used to have eyes. I think of the time Ella gouged out a doll's eyes on Christmas morning and put them in her pocket. Does she have the doll eyes with her wherever she is now?

Now the Machine rams into the wall, pounding against our house. I'm thrown out of my wheelchair and land next to Father beneath the table. The walls shake, but they haven't yet collapsed, and we haven't yet been exterminated.

A good drops from above. Maybe someone threw it in through the chimney. I crawl over to fetch it, but it slides away across the now sloping floor. I reach out after it. Is it a gift?

Little by little, we all slide sideways. The good slides, too. It's wrapped in cellophane. Father throws the doll high up into the air, and it flies out of the chimney. Mother and I watch it disappear.

Here we are, slipping sideways, the three of us, Mother, Father and me. The good rolls on past us, and this time I manage to grab hold of it. I look at the label. It's a pre-cut chicken, with a brown face nestled between the drumsticks.

A child with black hair. The child's mouth is agape, and staring out at me from behind the cellophane is a pair of terrified eyes.

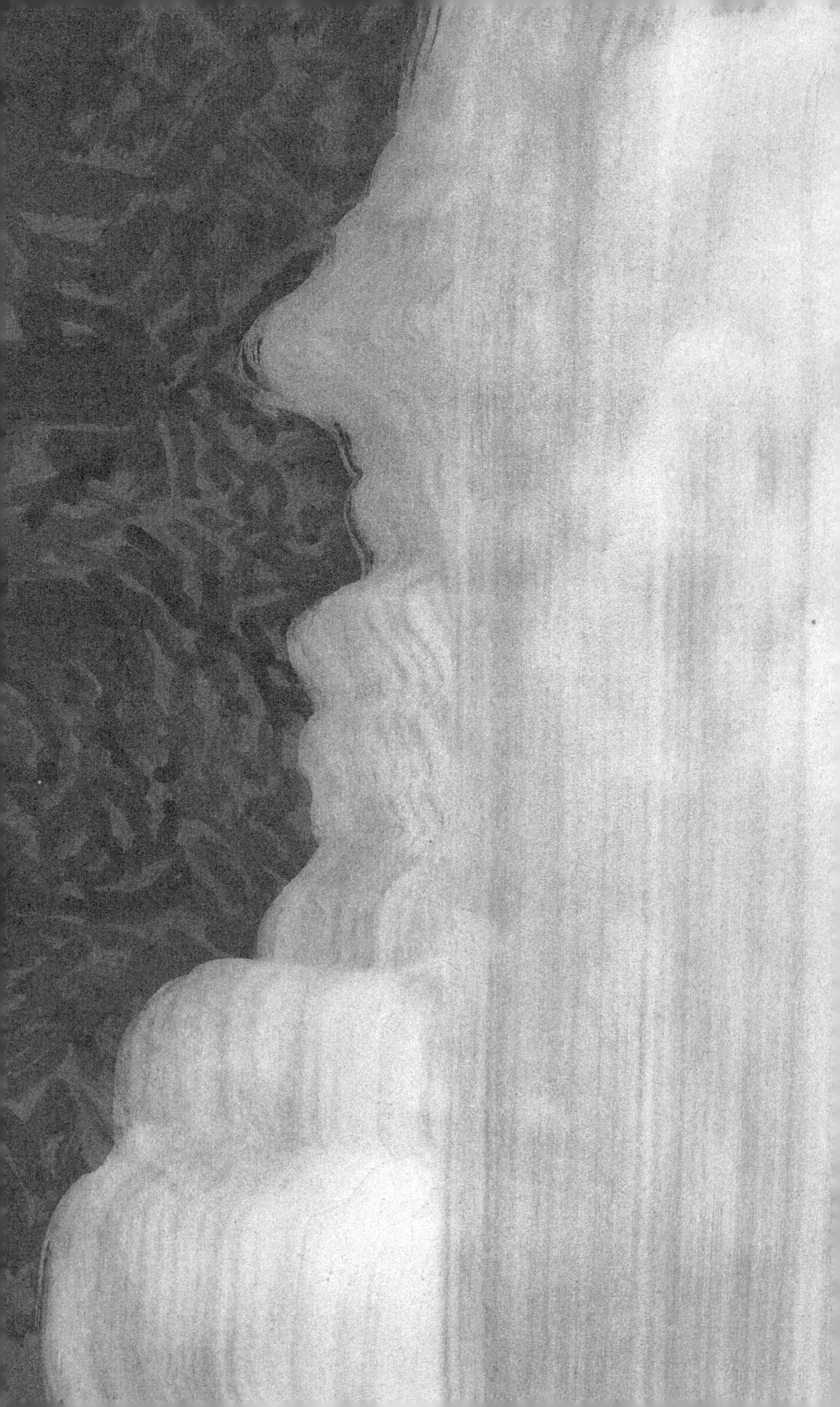

To Russia
Ermelunden Forest, 1888

I was in my garden when the tunnel in Ermelunden collapsed. The tunnel collapsed, and I could see it from my garden. Julius, my partner, saw it too from where he stood outside in the mud. We're doomed, I thought out loud. Now everyone knows. We are the unsuccessful engineers. Then, even louder, I said: But this is your chance to leave. Your failure is an opportunity. Finally you can go to Russia!

An old supervisor stood on the muddy construction site with a smirk on his face, relishing in my misfortune. Niels Madsen's great tunnel, my great tunnel, had collapsed. I had failed to build a tunnel that could hold, and that delighted him.

I had gone into the house and was sitting by the window. The supervisor was still watching me from outside. He heard the shouts too, I thought. He's waiting to see how a person deals with their misfortune, slouching a little to appear indifferent, but he's staring at me, mocking me, laughing at me on the inside.

To my surprise, I didn't pass out, but calmly reached for the pot and poured myself some coffee with my eyes still fixed on the collapsed tunnel. My hands didn't tremble. I didn't feel depressed. I wanted to go to Russia, the true fatherland, as Julius and I called it. The time has come to realise that dream, I thought. I was glad, in fact, because all along I had feared that things would go wrong with the tunnel. *If so, I'll leave,* I had told myself. And now it had happened. Jørgine was calling my name, and my daughter Klara came running into the kitchen from the garden. Father, you're stomping your feet, she said, pointing at my boots.

I fanned away a mosquito and laughed: I'm going to Russia, to Siberia, where the lakes are iced over. Where people are submerged beneath the frozen water and only their noses stick up. Like in Dante's *Inferno,* where the souls of the punished get trapped beneath the ice...

I sang: That's us, the unsuccessful engineers, Niels and Julius, who will be punished in frozen lakes. Julius and me. Yes, I'm off to the place where Danes truly belong. To Russia.

It was an impulse we'd had, Julius and I. Many before us had gone to Russia to uncover the proud, glorious culture concealed behind the myth of the gruesome empire. We believed that Danes have belonged with the Russians since the dawn of time, and we ought to go there, learn from their ways and mingle with the many peoples of Eastern Russia, where 40 different languages are spoken.

Klara watched me from her perch in the windowsill with a bowl in her hands. I laughed like someone sentenced to the gallows who tries to put on a brave face while their child is looking on. Klara hopped down and dropped the bowl. It was full of sand, which sprinkled across my feet. She disappeared into the living room just as Julius came walking up to the house and stopped outside the window.

We talked as we had so many times before, from either side of the window ledge. Often we would talk for ages. But now that I knew he too had watched our masterpiece, the tunnel, collapse, I just wanted to get it over with. I was tired of it all, I realised, including him. Tired of watching the rain and sleet and waiting for friends with whom I rarely laughed, tired of the misery that seemed to descend from the sky in this country. All winter long, it was difficult to tell the sky from the ground. It seemed to me I had never belonged in this country, and Julius, whom I called my friend, looked like a stranger with his red nose and reddish beard, and I thought: I'm not taking him with me to Russia. I want to start over on my own! I was only listening to his lengthy monologue with half an ear. No one will blame us for the accident, Julius said, and even if they do, all is not lost. We can still continue our work.

But the tunnel is gone, I thought. It collapsed, the tunnel we've dreamt of completing for years. The tunnel which was the final step in the government's plan to artificially flood the region in the event of foreign invasion, preventing the enemy from reaching the capital. Had the tunnel not collapsed, the city's line of defence would have been complete. But now we've made a mess of both flood and defence lines with our botchwork of a tunnel, our tunnel which ended up collapsing, I thought. I felt nauseous in the back of my throat. A stabbing pain in my stomach. Julius ambled about outside, oddly cheerful.

The old supervisor passed by in the distance with gold buttons on his coat. He pretended not to see us. Then he turned around, suddenly in a rush. His coat buttons gleamed in a flash of sunlight.

It was the evening of March 23rd, Julius had left and I found myself suddenly in high spirits. I went out into the forest and sat on the trunk of a fallen tree. From here, I could look out at both our house and the collapsed tunnel without being noticed. A bluish smoke hovered above the roof, and I began to have doubts as to whether I dared to journey out on my own. You look like a ghost, Niels. People would think you had fled, Julius had told me.

Early the next morning, before the doubts could crop up, I left.

I could hear shouts in the distance from the workers out by the collapsed tunnel. I had never lived with anyone as long as I had with my wife Jørgine, but I didn't say goodbye when I left our bed. It was still full of the sand Klara had scattered across the blankets that time when she slept in it. She had left pebbles and seashells beneath our pillows. I staggered through the village as though seasick. My old stomach pains had returned, setting fire to my gut. The pain radiated up into my arms, shot through my legs, and it didn't stop. Already I missed the coffee Jørgine served each morning in the cosy kitchen I had just left behind. I thought of little things, my slippers, and the steam that always formed on the kitchen windows when the kettle boiled. But I had to leave.

I pressed on. The street was dry. I set out through the forest. As I walked, I realised I was unsure of where to go. Should I go to Copenhagen and stay there? Or continue on from there to Russia? I stayed in my uncertainty, but my feet moved in only one direction: I was approaching my childhood home, a few kilometres from the house I shared with Jørgine and Klara.

What if the old house is empty? I thought. I could sleep in the stable like I used to as a kid.

For years I had steered clear of my childhood home, and yet I had never stopped orbiting around it.

I stopped at the cemetery on the way and sat down beside a grave to rest for a while, listening to my heart, which always surprised me with its strong, steady beat. I looked at the windswept yellow wheat beyond the chain link fence and the never-changing seagulls, which looked like splatters of paint in the sky. Far off in the distance, I could still hear the shouts of the workers presumably still gathered around the collapsed tunnel. I lay down in the shadows of the graveyard's bulbous plants and covered my ears like I used to back when my mother was dying. Often when I stood with my hands clamped over my ears, staring at my mother asleep in her bed, my sister would sneak up behind me. She would pry my hands from my hot ears and wash them with a warm washcloth, whispering to me: I'll make tea. And then we would go out to the stable, and drink our tea by the horses softly munching in the dark.

It would soon be morning. A thick fog surrounded the grave on which I lay shivering. I had sacrificed everything for the tunnel, I thought, I had been worn down, humiliated and ridiculed for building it, and now, out of shame, I have fled. What must the others think of me? Do they consider me a coward? Before I could dwell any further on the humiliation and fear of being remembered as a coward, the sky began to brighten beyond the trees. The fog lifted. I stood up from the grave and continued with sure steps towards my childhood home, but when I reached the well at the edge of the garden, I stopped.

I climbed down into the well. For two days, I hid inside it.

Once in a while I would climb back up and spy into the rooms of my parents' old house. I could see a woman my age moving around in there. She dusted and cooked as though expecting a visitor for lunch.

After nightfall, I snuck up all the way to the house. Walked around in the old stable, which now stood nearly empty. There was just a single horse, still munching in the dark just like when I was little. I found a couple of blankets, water from the trough, a few loaves of bread in the storeroom next to the stable, and brought it all back to the well. Then the stomach ache set in. I lay in the well biting back the pain and gazed up at the rustling pines.

The forest above me was growing light. I chewed on some bread crusts, thinking about my boyhood in the house. Just 20 metres away lay the place where I had been served glasses of almond milk before bed. I remembered the ginger scent of our morning tea. I thought about it more and more. The pain intensified, and so did the memories: the blue of my mother's glass in the window. The jar of cinnamon.

I almost hoped Jørgine would appear and say: I know where you are. I know you. I want to be with you, no matter where. We'll run away, together.

20 years ago, after my mother died, I had run away from my childhood home and left my father and sister behind. As I fled through the forest, a stomach ache had forced me to stop and rest along the way, but before long the pain subsided and I had made it all the way to Copenhagen on

foot. Now I could feel how my body had aged. Back then, I had lived off what I found along the way; roots and berries, apples, mushrooms. And that had suited me just fine.

I climbed out of the well and walked down the familiar path to the house. Inside those rooms I had dreamed up plans as a boy, before I ran away. The woman I had been watching the past few days was kneeling in the garden, planting potatoes.

Have a handful, she whispered, and to be polite I accepted the sprouting tubers. No, she said, don't tell anyone. You know how worked up people get when it comes to the homeless! Hospitality is a crime in this country, so you're best to stay away, she said.

The woman in the potato patch told me her name was Maja, like the sister I abandoned 20 years ago. Maja, she said, shaking my hand, and then she pointed at her dog. She whistled and called for it: Paradiso. That's its name, she said. A strange name for a dog, I thought. Paradiso! The soil became more pungent when the dog came racing across it to the woman. A craving for coffee urged me closer; perhaps we could have a little chat inside?

The front door stood open. I lingered outside, peering into the hallway. There were pictures of singing angels on the walls. I wondered whether she was a widow. She returned with a cup of coffee and thanked the fates that allowed her to help the homeless! After all, the nights are still cold in March. Everyone needs food and a roof over their heads. She gave me permission to smoke, and I took a walk around her house, which was screaming for a fresh coat of paint.

Was she childless? She had planted too many roses in my opinion.

As I stood behind the house, I saw that she had gone into the kitchen. I watched her through the window for a while as she sliced bread, sawing at it with the dull side of the blade. I recognised that mistake! It's her, I thought. That's my sister. She never left. She still lives here. I wanted to run inside and cry 'sister', but I hesitated. What if she mentioned our father? I debated. A moment later, it was too late.

I turned away from the window and the sight of Maja buttering bread. I listened to the chatter of ducks in a nearby pond and watched a cloud take form and dissolve again. Then Maja called for me. She served coffee and bread in the sitting room. The clouds drew their hood over the sky. The horse whinnied in the stable.

I didn't look at her. I told myself: Yes, we were once family, but people change. I asked whether there was a stable here, just to say something, and she pointed to it. I stood up and walked over with the coffee cup in my hand. She followed me and let me clean the horse's hooves and scatter hay, she let me feed it and clean the stable.

The horse's hooves were tangled in grass and caked in mud, and for the first time in years I mucked out. I felt free. She let me help her. Does she recognise me after all, but is hiding it like I am? I wondered. I didn't know. And I still wasn't in Russia. I had made it no further than to my childhood home, yet it had taken me 20 years to get here. I shivered in the stable and thought: Tomorrow I'll tell her that we're siblings, but I knew I had to wait for the right moment.

She told me several times that her name was Maja, and each time she said it I stared stiffly ahead and did not react. I was named after my mother, who died much too soon, she said, and I kept her name, because it was her who wanted me to have it.

Maja spoke only little of her childhood, and in broad strokes. She had once had a little brother who ran away from home after their mother's death, and she had been living in the house on her own ever since. I didn't ask whether she had thought of her brother over the years, and she made no mention of her father. It would seem he hadn't been around since her mother died and her little brother ran away.

Maja stood up.

I need a little hut to seek shelter in, she said, and told me about a delegation from the fortifications of Copenhagen. They had stopped by six months ago to inform her that the state was planning an artificial flood to keep out the enemy, and that her property might be flooded, making her house uninhabitable. There will be lots of water, she said, raising her arms to show me. They plan to unleash the water and let it surge through all the new dams on Zealand to keep the enemy at bay. When the water comes, I plan to move to higher grounds!

So I've long wanted to build a hut, she said, with room for the horse, too. I didn't want to tell her that the work on the fortification and their plans to artificially flood parts of Zealand were probably put on hold.

Maja hauled tools out into the courtyard and lugged a bucket up the little hill in the garden. After lunch I got to work sawing planks, and it felt like a furious farewell song about the extraordinary artificial flood. Which would have been possible, had my tunnel not collapsed.

Maja's voice was glum: I'd rather stay, even though they tell me I should move out of the house, she said.

A moment of silence. Then she spat out her words; words of anger against the state that wanted her to leave her home. The cursed idea of building forts and fortifications to keep out enemies who never come anyway, she sneered. Driving people out of their homes for fear of someone there's likely no reason to fear. No, I've changed my mind. I won't be moving to higher grounds. I'm staying put, she insisted. Let the water come and take me. Yes, let the house be flooded! She laughed: *If* the enemy comes, that is.

Then I heard her heavy footfalls across the gravel. She had gone to fetch more coffee and milk, and I clattered on with the construction all the way until dark.

She got out a folding chair for each of us and set them up on the hill. In the darkness you could see other hills, giving off their heavy steam. She hung her scarf on the first and only wall I had built. Her way of asking me something, with food extended in offering, made me want to throw my arms around her. At that moment she looked just the same as when she was a little girl.

It was quiet in Maja's house. Much quieter than back home by the now collapsed tunnel in Ermelunden. Back when I lived there, people would often ask me questions, and my vision would blur as they waited for my response, which I usually could not think of. The supervisor had kept a vigilant eye on me, like a hawk waiting for a mouse to scamper forth from the leaves.

He had delighted in my greatest mistake: My tunnel really had collapsed. Julius's and my tunnel had turned into a burial pit, and I had known my family and I would be sent away, utterly destitute. But perhaps if I leave, I thought, they would get help from the state or from Julius, so that's what I had done. I left for their sake, I was on my way to Russia, and had not brought anyone with me.

One morning we burned hymnals in the garden, Maja and I. The pages of the hymnals which had been passed down from Father's childhood at a vicarage whirled about in the air. Bits of paper rose up in a column of smoke like little birds and scattered across the landscape. Maja sat down on a tree stump beside the fire, and said: That's how the man who died in Ermelunden will be burned, too.

What man in Ermelunden? I asked, tossing some twigs and dry leaves onto the fire. Every now and again the fire threatened to die out, it had grown chilly, the sun had already vanished behind the hills. I prodded at the fire with a stick to stoke the embers. It sputtered. I wiped soot from my face. Our coats were two mute souls draped across a tree stump.

What man from Ermelunden? I asked again, still watching the fire, and put on my blue coat. The morning light flowed into me like new blood. I glanced down at myself, wiped my brow, and my neck and arms. Eventually it became difficult to remain quiet. What man from Ermelunden? I asked once more. We couldn't find anything else to burn, now only embers were left, slowly devouring the hymnals, and then, shielding her eyes, she said softly: It's the engineer, Niels Madsen. They say he drowned himself. They're burying him today.

Maja tore off through the garden, and I chased after her, grabbing her by the shoulders. Don't, she whispered.

I spun around. Now Maja was over by the fire. She turned to face me with a look of triumph in her eyes. I turned my back to her. I'm going to Russia, I declared, and instead of going inside for lunch, I ran towards the forest. After a while I slowed down, realising there was no real threat. I almost smiled. I searched for a distinctive scent in the air or the sound of an animal, but there was nothing. The air was still as the sea. Not a breeze stirred, it must have been around ten in the morning, and the fields and the forest were bathed in a limpid light.

So people thought I was dead! They were under the impression that I was rotting up in a boat at the bottom of the sea. That was the rumour circulating. Maja had read about it in the newspaper: a young worker from Ermelunden was certain he had seen me, Niels Madsen, pushing a boat into the water the day I disappeared. He claimed to have seen me headed out to sea in a tiny dinghy in a storm!

The church bells tolled in the distance, the flag was at half-mast.

The day of what everyone believed to be my funeral had arrived, that's what Maja had said. I sat on a rock in the forest, unable to bring myself to set out.

I thought back to when my mother was dying. Her body had taken up such little space in the bed. For the first time in years I could see her, perfectly and clearly. Then I recalled the six windows that were opened in the church tower, one on each side, when my father, who worked at the church, struck the copper bell again and again. He had given the world sound with the power of his hands. His hands had worked with the greatest of ease, sending the bells clanging back and forth.

There on the rock, I also remembered the look my father gave me just after my mother took her last breath. He, my sister and I had gathered our chairs around my mother's bed in the living room. His eyes had changed in an instant, and for a moment he had two faces. Then the new face won over and his smile was gone. He glared at me from my mother's bedside, full of spite. I never found out what he was thinking at that moment. What had gone through his mind.

Another memory came to me, of the day that preceded my leaving home. I brought only a few things with me. After packing, I had slept in my mother and father's big bed. My final night. The house was cold. I had clutched the duvet and listened for sounds from my father, who in the time after my mother's death had got into the habit of wandering in and out of the house at night. That night I hadn't known where my sister and father had gone, and when I got thirsty, I didn't dare go downstairs on my own. Not until dawn did I venture down. It had no longer felt like my home, although on the surface everything remained the same. The cold had taken over the house, as though a great big grave had forced its way through the walls. On the kitchen table stood my mother's coffin.

While I sat on the rock listening to the church bells ring, I felt a kind of guilt over being alive, here, just a few kilometres from where they were about to lower my coffin into the ground. A coffin with nothing inside it, because people believed my body to be at the bottom of the sea.

Eventually I ran onwards through the forest to witness my funeral. It wasn't too late yet. The church bells were still ringing. The path towards Ermelunden was muddy. A long stretch of mire which felt like it was endless. My trousers got soaked when I waded through a lake to reach the church faster.

Between the church and the cemetery stood a cluster of tall pines. The church bells were still ringing. They sang inside my head. I approached the pine closest to the church.

I placed my foot on the tree's bottom branch and began to climb as though ascending a stairway of dry branches. Not once did I tread on a brittle branch; I climbed as were it the most natural thing in the world. Once in a while I leaned back against the trunk to gain my bearings, and my feet soon became ice-cold. All I had were my feet and my hands, no rope to secure to the top. I had never known how a person climbs such a tall tree. Finally I found myself among the spindly branches of the very top, where the footing was poor.

From here, I could look directly into the church's nave. I watched the service through the windows, my funeral service. 40 or 50 people had turned up. I strained to hear the priest's sermon. Jørgine had put on her black bonnet. She greeted Julius. His eyes were narrow between his temples. The church bell tolled not far from me. I kept trying to focus on other things, not the fact that it was my coffin over which they were singing in the church. A coffin without me inside it.

Then they exited in a procession that made its way between crosses and winter aconite. I followed them with my eyes as they walked along the graves. Julius was smoking.

The sun stopped shining. Julius kissed Jørgine's hand and closed his eyes, leaning in closer. Then the yellow May sun reappeared, lighting up the pit of the gravesite. The priest avoided the words 'by his own hand', but mentioned 'the power of the sea', 'death by drowning, which takes many unfortunate fathers', 'the bereft children and wives'. The rain began to fall as a heavy, grey veil onto the mourners at my grave.

It was late May, and I watched them lower the coffin into the ground and throw soil on top. I saw the whole thing while hidden from view in the treetops' dense green foliage. I felt a twinge in my stomach. I don't have to be lonely, I thought. Suddenly I longed for peril and foes. I didn't climb down to the others. Why not? No. I couldn't.

To Russia! I sang so softly no one below could hear me, just to remind myself. After they buried me, there would be no going back. That's what I thought. I would become a new person! Soon they would all finally understand me. I would send them a letter from Russia telling them everything: that I was alive, that I would one day return for my wife and my daughter.

But for now I had freed myself from them, like when you fight your way out of a bramble and find yourself very suddenly released from the thorns' grip! As I made my way back to Maja's house, I felt furious that I had not dropped everything sooner and gone to Russia long ago.

The door clattered behind me. I rushed into the living room. Maja was waiting for me. In a few days I'll set out for Russia, I shouted. Will you be upset? I asked, and she didn't answer. Why did the announcement make me feel so calm, even though I had neither money nor ticket and no idea where to find help when I arrived?

Maja walked out to the front of the house, humming a tune, and when she turned back to me and smiled, I noticed that she had cut off all her hair while I was gone. The remaining tufts were the colour of stone and stuck straight out of her scalp, very fine and short. I couldn't help but stare at her figure, transfixed. It was as though she had wanted to alter herself so entirely I would no longer be able to recognise her.

That night I lay listening to the wind in the trees. I remembered my humiliation in Ermelunden and thought: I'll seek work when I get to Eastern Russia. I'll learn multiple of the 40 languages spoken there. I'll live in the forest. Pick berries and gather moss. I'll write books. How would they possibly discover a Dane among so many different peoples? Most importantly, I'll forget all about my former life.

People had once called my work as an engineer fantastic: Niels Madsen's dedication is fantastic! But it wasn't. My work was nothing but fanaticism in its purest form. My attempt to avoid this unease and tedium had been doomed from the start. I should never have taken on the job in Ermelunden. I should have left 20 years ago, I told myself. After my mother died, when my father transformed in a single night. The night he turned evil.

And so I lay in bed ruminating in this manner. There was lightning, and it started to rain. I couldn't fight the feeling of a band of steel around my skull. The public humiliation of the tunnel collapsing was still ripping my thoughts to shreds. I hoped to wake up in Russia and find myself the person I was as a child, before my home turned evil because my father did. After my humiliation, I never wanted to see Ermelunden again.

A sudden sickness and daze kept me in bed at Maja's for an entire month after the funeral. Maja gave me horse chestnuts and baking soda and told me to rub my body with vinegar to soothe my nerves. I gave my little brother the same treatment once, she told me. Every night my little brother would ask my mother and me: Will you still be here when I wake up? He always feared that disaster would strike at night, she said. One time, in jest, our mother told him no. That sent my brother into hysterics, Maja said.

I lost all sensation in my legs when Maja told me that story. I reached out my hands as a way of telling her it was me. She stood up and I told her my legs were asleep, and she said they needed a vinegar bath. Yes, he certainly was an anxious one, my little brother, she went on, sweeping her gaze across the garden outside. I said nothing and accepted the vinegar she brought me.

For days I did not dare think of Russia. The stomach ache persisted, but I began to regain movement in my legs. I lay beneath a blanket. We would often sit in silence in the evening, sensing the garden's stillness. 20 years had passed uneasily. But in the days I was bedridden at Maja's, although I was too sick to stand upright, I felt calm.

You have the kind of teeth angels have, Maja chuckled one evening shortly before midnight. We were sitting in the living room. Angels, I laughed. So did my little brother, she said. They have special teeth, angels, did you know that? I've seen angels many times in my life. Easily seven times, if not more. How? I asked, and I hoped that here, in the dark, she would say aloud the thing I was certain she knew. I hoped she would say: You're my little brother.

Angels have much bigger teeth than humans, she said.

That night I dreamt I met Jørgine at an inn with our daughter. They appeared foreign to me, two young women dressed in black with their blonde hair done up. Their eyes unrecognisable. Too big. Crazed. Stomping, shivering, reproachful women. Say something, one of them shouted at me. Answer, why don't you, Niels! They glanced at each other, and my daughter whimpered: He's terrible! Then they made as if to leave and galloped through the revolving door like two horses riding out of my life.

While I was sick, I remembered how illness had roused like an animal in the house when my mother was dying, slowly and stealthily, wedging itself between my parents. I remembered the broken cups, the peculiar pauses in their speech, the cries of pain from the room next to the kitchen. My father had skirted around my mother's room as if she were a demon carrying an insidious infection.

Only death surpassed illness in its ability to tear people apart. Death was not, as many claimed, something you learned from, something that brought you closer. No, fatal illness meant strained conversations. Mother had lain in an impenetrable fortress, the thicket around her room growing denser year after year. She had been bored and suffered splitting headaches. All she ever wanted was to sleep, she longed to cry herself to sleep, to death – perhaps precisely because she had never been able to cry, her eyes always dry and alert.

Maja came in to see how I was doing. She handed me a cup of tea and asked whether we should go drink it with the horse in the stable. I felt certain she was beginning to understand why, of all places, it was at her doorstep I had shown up in late March of this year. I told her I was freezing. I'll take care of that, she said.

Maja passed by outside in the garden with a shovel over her shoulder; she did everything on her own now that I was sick.

Later I hugged her, and said: Thank you! But she didn't move, didn't return my embrace. She stared at me. Said nothing. I could hear the clock strike 12 in the living room.

She offered to show me how to use her stove, told me how long the tea had to steep, that sort of thing. Meanwhile I watched a pair of rabbits in the garden. They resembled two chess pieces, one black and one white. It made me laugh. Imagine, said Maja, that man in Ermelunden. Someone finally found his remains washed up on a beach. I searched her face in the dark. For a long time we sat in silence, tense. The door was left ajar, should someone suddenly want out.

You must keep away from wine, keep away from coffee and sugar, I told myself. I longed for Russia, for places even colder and darker than here.

I saw an obituary for Niels Madsen in the newspaper. And articles about a trial over his suicide.

Every time my vision blurred, I felt as though winds were rushing through the room and I was convinced I saw my daughter Klara standing outside the window. Soon it would be July. Each morning I did knee bends on the lawn. Took cold baths. Rubbed my skin in goose fat. It helped. In my feverish state of exhaustion, the old furniture and books in the house began to repulse me. I felt the compulsion to get rid of it all so I could search behind the furniture for a rotten apple. Like at the house in Ermelunden, where I had once torn an entire cabinet off the wall to figure out why it smelled of mould, but there was nothing there.

I dreamt that my daughter came to visit. Her hair was completely white. She died very abruptly in my arms, and I felt a deep sense of guilt. She turned into an urn of sand that fell to the floor and shattered into a thousand pieces.

It was late morning. I awoke to tea and my sister's troubled brown eyes. Why was she making me tea yet again this morning? She handed me the cup and took a seat, following my movements while she ran her fingers through her cropped grey hair. I limped up and down the dirty, dusty stairs at the back of the house to fetch flour for baking bread, and Maja looked at me, waiting, as I set the sack of flour on the kitchen floor.

The garden was pleasantly windy. She sent me outside to relax, telling me she needed to take care of some things in the house. If only I had money for the journey, I thought as I sat on the bench. I wrote a list: Chocolate. Ginger. Cinnamon. Milk bread. Twine. Wool. The gold jewellery.

Each day I feared Julius would show up here and expose me, revealing that I was still alive, and I would be punished for having lied about my death. The resurrected Niels, the liar, the man who ran away.

The day grew hotter as the hours passed. Julius had probably gone back to work at Ermelunden, I thought.

I went back inside and took out the old blueprint of the tunnel from 1886 I had brought with me so I could suffer the way I eventually would in purgatory. I studied a map of Ermelunden Hill for a long time. Had we thought too highly of ourselves? That's how God cuts the prideful down to size, I thought. But that was just another excuse. Everyone had always known the tunnel might collapse. And yet right up to the very end we had gone on digging, intent on showing the world that we could be the first to complete the tunnel through Ermelunden Hill. We even raved about medals, we did.

Afterwards I went down to the living room. Maja wasn't there. I thought I had to be dreaming. The house was empty. On the table was a note.

I've gone on ahead, Little Brother.

Maja had gone to Russia.

Notpla's House

I'll tell the story, even if no one is listening: A shadow trailed after me the other day. It appeared in glimpses, one moment to my right, the next to my left. I kept on nervously turning around to look for it as I walked. Suddenly, it was gone. It must have been someone who lost their way, I thought... I kept looking for the shadow. It could have been someone out to kill me.

A few hours later, I ran into it again.

The shadow caught me off guard, leaping out from its hiding behind a tree, scratching my face and pinning my arm behind me. I managed to break free of its grip and backed away. The shadow stood menacingly in front of me, wielding its water bottle like a weapon. It wore a rabbit mask over its face. Is that you? I asked. We'll see, it said.

I think I arrived at the house at night. Notpla was here to greet me, drinking coffee in a wicker chair in front of the house. The porch light spotlighted his feet. It was snowing, but he was wearing sandals. Notpla jumped up and practically screamed: Finally, you're here! For 40 years I've missed you!

Our embrace. Could you call it an embrace? His breath smelled rancid. As he hugged me, the light became nauseatingly bright. He squinted at me. I think we took a few dance steps. Did we levitate?

Notpla lived in the old house. Right away I was inclined to believe that I had finally come *home*, and that Notpla was a guardian of sorts. We went inside. From the kitchen came a strong smell of boiled ham. In the living room, flies buzzed about in the ceiling. There were only the most necessary furnishings: a table, a computer, a rug, a sofa, and from the ceiling hung a bare light bulb.

It was quiet. I looked out the window. The lawn was strewn with coffee cups, and the moon above was only just discernible, a grey half-disc in the fog. I studied the floor. Its wooden planks were patterned with shapes resembling plants, and roots, reeds, shoots, flowers, stems, tissue. All of it carved in the greatest of detail.

Among the floral patterns I could also make out shapes resembling child hands and wrinkled skin. Others looked like corals, vines, eyelashes. As I studied the floor, Notpla washed my clothes. Then he draped my towels and dresses over the backs of chairs to dry and lit a fire in the stove.

The sky rumbled like usual.

Something barbaric is in store, I thought. Or is it already over?

It doesn't really sound as though there's a war going on, but it *is* possible that I sought shelter at Notpla's to escape a war. Is that why I'm so quiet? If that's the case, am I the enemy? And is Notpla my ally? I have memories of the shadow, my stalker. Could that have been my enemy?

It's best to breathe inaudibly and keep the lights off so

as not to be discovered. From the murky house, I can see the fields, the church, the road. Notpla moves about in my vicinity. I can detect his fishy breath. Coffee, he roars. When I say coffee, that means there's coffee!

Gradually, I start to see him more clearly. He's oddly broad-shouldered, despite his small stature. His eyes are blue, and one eye is slightly bigger than the other. He moves his lips and speaks, but I can't hear him. It's as though the sea has lodged itself in my ears, or as though Nopla is speaking a foreign language. I stare intently at his pink tongue and the movements of his lips, his brownish teeth. He peers out at the rose bed blooming in the dark with narrowed eyes, then falls silent.

The cemetery and my former life don't simply feel distant, it's as though they never existed. I belong here now, everything is new again. I'm discovering this home for the first time, and I get lost in it.

I hum. Notpla sits in his chair. His blue eye blinks restlessly. His eyelashes flutter like the tails of cows swatting flies in the summer heat.

He catches sight of me and smiles in surprise, as though we haven't had eye contact for a long time. It smells of soil and skin. The trees rustle in the wind. Suddenly Notpla starts to sob: I miss... something, he murmurs with trembling lips.

Massacres, he whispers, pounding his fist on the table. Don't assume I'll forget what happened in...

He's silent for a moment, and I scarcely know what to think or do. The distant look in his eyes remains unchanged. I notice that my vision is slightly blurry, as it often is.

We sit in the house together, gazing out at the boats in the garden. My vision has cleared up again. The boats are waiting for an answer, but they won't get it, I think. Green boats. Red boats. I'll stop speaking, I decide. It's the same thing every time, and now I'll say no more. I live in the house I found. Notpla's house. That's all there is to it. He takes care of me.

The grooves in the boats' hulls look like ears straining to listen. I keep coming back to look at the boats. I have a feeling they've been there since I was born. A couple of bottles swim about in the red boat, half sunken, scraping the bottom. The green boat is turned on its back. A fishing net tacked to its surface flaps in the wind.

Bird cries from high above fly through the wind. We hear the distant quacking of ducks in a marsh. The afternoon's last light falls on Notpla.

I've been dozing. A draught blows across my shoulders and neck. Notpla raises his voice when he speaks to me, so I do the same. That's the way it is here. We have to drown out the room, which feels so foreign even though it's all I remember, this room, my home. Is there a forest here? I shout. Notpla responds shrilly: No, there's no forest. Only the trees in the garden.

The flies buzz about. They've multiplied. Dead flies on the floor and lazy flies in the ceiling. It's quieted down. There's a looming sense of catastrophe. What might have happened here before my return? I wonder. Once in a while Notpla will mention arson. Massacres in the forest. People on the run. There are fish on my plate. Who fried them? The flies nibble at them. The legs of the flies move across the fish sandwiches.

Birds chirp in the bushes outside. I laugh, realising it's only a memory. Then I weep, silently, without tears. I've always been fond of birdsong. It comes to me in my memories. Always the same birdsong. My hearing is so poor I can't tell whether the birds out there really are chirping softly in the trees.

I lose myself in the boats again. Boats aren't out of their minds, I think. They don't degenerate the way humans do. Boats know nothing of the blood that can thicken and clot in human veins. A boat doesn't die. But Notpla and I, we do.

Notpla walks with a cane now. He didn't when I first arrived. His neck is limp, and his head droops to one side. He looks at me with disappointment. My breath is slow and belaboured. The wind flings open the front door and blows right into the living room. The door is open – should someone suddenly want out. It goes straight to my bones.

The moonlight falls across the boats, making them look like half globes. I should bring a boat inside one of these days. It would be reassuring to have a boat ready in the house. I feel as though I'm all alone now. Each morning when I wake, I'm convinced time has been turned back to 1999.

The corn stalks are rotting in the fields this winter, the warmest winter ever, and the seagulls sit on the soft ground in pools of their own vomit. The starry night sky quivers hotly above Notpla's house. A bird crashes into the little window of our house and breaks its neck. I'm afraid of the moon. My heavy body, back and forth in this little house. My raspy breath, like a branch scraping a bucket. The bulb in the half-shattered porch light glares.

This March it will be 20 years ago, Notpla says. But it's only been 12 years, I think. Next thing he claims it's been 40 years since the disasters began. Since the epidemic broke out. It all started with that woman, he insists with a smug look. She was a devil. You hear me? The window panes clatter when he pounds his fist against the top of his black lacquer desk. If you only knew what she did to us all.

What woman, Notpla? I ask.

The frost arrives very suddenly. The darkness wraps itself like a noose around my tongue. Notpla towers up in the centre of the room dressed in a dark green coat. I think he's about to say something more about the epidemic and the woman, but he doesn't.

Notpla moaned all night long. This morning, his leg has turned black. He seems proud as he points to his leg and wails: Look, my leg is completely black!

He uses his black leg as an excuse. He doesn't go to the kitchen to make coffee or a roast. He leans back, hitches up his trousers and dolefully regards his leg. Then he sighs, strokes the taut, black skin and rolls his trousers back down. He doesn't take notice of the fridge or the stove. The old potatoes in the pot. The stench of rotten meat in the oven. He goes to sit on the porch in the glow of the sole lamp out there. I don't know whether or not to call him inside. The sky rumbles like usual.

So there are people here after all. A crowd has queued up in front of the church on the hill beyond the fields. I suppose they're waiting to climb to safety up into the church tower. The two of us watch them. Someone is already up top and opens the windows of the six-sided steeple. We can't see the bell from here, but we know it's there. Big, and made of copper.

I expect to hear the sound of a bell ringing any minute, but none comes. Notpla doesn't move. He stares into space. Why doesn't the bell ring? he suddenly exclaims. It must be long after eight o'clock. I'm always waiting to hear whether he'll go on speaking. Neither of us can take our eyes off the light from the church.

I feel tired, and I break a bar of chocolate in half. It's nearly nine. I eat one square of dark chocolate after the next and realise that I can clear my mind that way.

All at once, something about the sight of the white birds getting tossed about in the storm like splatters of paint invigorates me. I want to laugh at the animals with Notpla, but he's fallen asleep at his computer.

I can see the rooftops of the village houses in the bright light outside. I tell myself this is a sight I want to tell the people back home about, when I eventually return to them. But what 'this' is I no longer remember, and with a shudder I realise that I may have forgotten everything before I reach them. Most likely I won't ever tell anyone about Notpla and the house, because it's questionable whether I have any other home than this one. So really, he's the person I'll eventually tell the story. I tie a scarf over my eyes and just listen to the storm.

The sky has taken on a greyish hue outside the window. The icicles are thawing. I feel as though I'm asleep for a moment as I observe everything around me. Notpla looks at me with a smile on his lips, the kind of smile you give an old dog.

His hair flutters over his green coat.

Notpla opens the door and goes outside. He stops and talks to someone on the phone. The sky takes on a dark-purple hue outside the window. As though a comet were about to land on the road.

A fishing rod topples onto my feet. I open my eyes. I had dozed off against the wall. The war can't get to us in here. The boats are roped together in the garden, gently rocking in the wind. Then everything vanishes in the rain, as though evil had seeped in.

Notpla is standing in the middle of the room with his trousers rolled up. The clouds have slipped off the sky. The hair on his head has grown. I've put on my cold slippers. I came running downstairs from my room to look at him. Far off on the fields, someone feeds an animal and empties a bucket of water into a trough. Good morning, I yell, watching Notpla, who doesn't answer. I fill the kettle and press the button. We regard one another. When are we having roast? he asks.

I've been expecting a crash all night long, and my skin is covered in scratches from my jittery nails. I've started scratching myself. The pill works a little, says Notpla, thank you. We look at each other and both fall quiet, as though something inside of us dies. There's a loud crash outside when a big, dead tree topples onto the hedge.

We sit in the armchairs. An insect lands on my cheek. Notpla's head droops forwards. The clock starts to irritate me, and I jiggle it out of the wall. It leaves behind a hole, and I check to see whether there's anything hidden inside, but there's nothing there.

The country is being depopulated, everyone's emigrating, Notpla snarls. Cowards. He tries to stand up, but his legs are stiff. There's a hard knock at the door. It's flung open. We turn around and see a pair of eyes gleaming in the dim corridor. Little Brother! He's alive, too. Winter is upon us again. And I have something to ask him. Little Brother has arrived unharmed, but I notice that his eyes are weary and edged with fine wrinkles.

Remember to disinfect your hands, Notpla yells, without looking at Little Brother. Here's a glass of water. And pills. How are you? He embraces Little Brother. Finally, you've returned, 40 years later, he hollers at him. I've disembarked, I'm doing better, says Little Brother and takes a sip of water.

Ten hours ago, Notpla's leg turned black, I whisper. My breathing makes a squeaking noise. Little Brother says: You talk too loudly! He turns on the TV. I must have forgotten to breathe, because the next moment I exhale lots of air in one go. Little Brother reaches for a towel. His eyelids move, but his cheeks and forehead remain frozen, and his hair, which was damp with heat when he arrived, is now dry. I hear myself whisper: Don't leave. Little Brother says: We need to chop the toppled tree up and drive it away.

Notpla has his eyes closed, lost in thought.

Notpla wants me to get up and blows smoke in my face to get me out of bed. He opens the window and flicks out the cigarette butt. Little Brother stands up and paces back and forth. Where do you shop around here? There are only pork loins in the freezer, he says. Are we meant to live off nothing but meat? I can't seem to form a reply. Notpla stares out into the darkness.

None of you move, says Little Brother. He takes out a camera and starts to film us. You look so alike! Then he puts his camera down and goes outside and fetches a wheelbarrow. Notpla gets up and watches Little Brother in the garden. Say, why is there a woman laughing at us through the window? he asks.

I sit up in bed and peer outside, but I can't see anyone. Has the epidemic reached us? Is Notpla sick?

Notpla wakes up on the sofa. It's always been essential that I remain on the island, he says, so when people started to leave, I resisted, dug in my heels, refused. Everyone has left, moved away, fled, since 1999.

My stomach hurts whenever you mention that year, I say. I'd rather go for a run. So why don't you just run to the church and back, Notpla sneers. Or across the fields! Notpla and Little Brother stand up simultaneously and both look out across the gravel. Their eyes wander down the road. They stare out at the porch light and the frothing clouds.

The sky often rumbles here on the island, I say. Have you noticed, Notpla? It's because of the space car, Notpla mumbles. That big white car, elongated, with no windows. It looks like a submarine on wheels driving past.

I know it's true, because I hear that car rumbling when I go to the toilet at night, but I don't tell Notpla that. Usually I rest my feet on the cold tiles and don't dare look out of the black windows when it cruises by. It's always the same:

That thing drives down the road, past our house. A space car that glides by almost inaudibly, as if underwater. Just a faint rumble, detectable only as a slight pressure on the skin. When it's nearby, it's impossible to tell whether it's the car, the garden or the sky that's rumbling.

Hide, Notpla orders. Everyone at the church can see you! I look at the birthmark beneath his eye. It seems to have migrated towards his ear.

The man I was fleeing had a birthmark just like that, remarks Little Brother, also studying Notpla's cheek. And the man in the church tower who pushed people out of the window had a birthmark beneath his eye too, he whispers. I ought to make a film about all those birthmarks.

It's already nine! Isn't there any breakfast, Notpla hollers. It's nearly midday!

Little Brother is watching Notpla through the lens of his camera. He doesn't miss a single movement. Notpla half-runs towards the kitchen. I pull my dress over my nightgown and trail after him. He stops in front of me with an empty coffee pot in his hand. Oh, there you are, he says. Always a shadow lurking in the doorway. You were like that as a child, too.

All the running has made him dizzy, and he closes his eyes and braces himself against the door. His shin is now less shiny and black, more violet.

While Notpla catches his breath, he sizes me up. On the whole you look the same as you did 40 years ago, he concludes. Then he starts to scream and shout, and his eyes grow round and expressionless. I turn away, moving my gaze from him to the wool blanket on the sofa and out at the frightening, almost colourless, grey branches of the pines. Notpla sighs.

I don't feel so well, I say. It's the same as back then, Notpla nods. You kids were always so feeble. You remember wrong, I say, it wasn't me who was sick all the time. That was your other child. He lashes out after me. You're all so mean, he whines. Why won't you just go along with the story? He sits down, sulking. Can't a person even get a cup of coffee in their own home anymore?

Notpla is speaking to a woman in front of the house. The woman says something. Notpla looks at her sullenly. The woman steps closer, and he turns away from her. Then he comes back inside the house. All three of us go stand by the window to watch her. She doesn't leave. The epidemic will start all over now, Notpla tells us. That woman and her children are evil. Look, she's staring at us. You must know, she's sick. Pretend not to see her. I hand him a blanket and suggest that he go rest on the sofa. He lets himself be persuaded to lie down and promptly falls asleep.

The wind that slips through the window offers no relief. It's humid and hot outside in the low light. The woman is still there. I look out at her through the black windows, sweating between my legs. The wind shakes the trees. My vision is blurry, as though a fog were hanging over the room. Then my vision clears. The trees and the church come into view. The woman is gone. My thighs are stuck together.

The wind blows the windows in the steppe open and shut. Little Brother is filming Notpla's sleeping face. Notpla certainly does look like the man in the tower, Little Brother whispers. You should have seen the man with Notpla's birthmark. He was dangerous. Believe me, he continues, glancing at Notpla. He didn't touch me, but he had a disease that made him throw women off the top of the church tower. There was no mercy. An entire ditch formed at the foot of the tower. A grave. That's where they landed. Other women would run out and bury them. What should we do?

I doze off. Little Brother carries on talking. I sit up. Now I hear him say: We ought to take another look at the man at the top of the church, just to be on the safe side. Cut into the birthmark, maybe. Keep an eye on what Notpla gets up to. That man, he followed many people all the way here. Those who got frightened sought shelter in the tower. He would rescue them. Afterwards he'd throw them off the top. I'll say this one last time: He looked a little bit like Notpla.

Two weeks at Notpla's house, and I still have no new acquaintances other than the woman. We live with Notpla on the deserted part of the island. Notpla took me in and gave me food and shelter. I can't remember meeting anyone other than Notpla since I came, apart from Little Brother, who arrived after I did. Is it possible that Notpla was the shadow who stalked me in the forest? Did he arrive just before I did? I can't stop thinking about the moment Little Brother arrived at Notpla's house, and Notpla exclaimed: I haven't seen you in 40 years. I don't mention that neither of us has turned 40. Only Notpla, who's at least twice my age.

The wind blows through the pines outside the window. In the dark, you can discern the contours of the chalk lines demarcating the basketball court on the field by the abandoned school. There's a barrel someone has attempted to burn rubbish in. Debris is strewn about all around it, old paintings, tools, soggy books and mouldy furniture.

Then I see her. The woman is right outside the window, mere centimetres away. She smoothes her hair and throws an anxious glance back towards the church, as though someone there is watching her. She looks at my hand on the window latch. Notpla is asleep. I open the window a crack. She extends her hand and tells me her name. I want to repeat it, but I can't, and instantly I've forgotten it. My stomach starts to ache terribly.

The woman shifts uneasily. She appears to be looking for a safe place to tread in the gravel. Leaves blow across the grass, crumpled and yellowed from too much sun. I curl my fingers. Do I mean her harm? I wait and listen. My fingers are still curled, but I don't know if I really want to hurt her, or anyone. It's as though my fingers are not mine, as though they have a will of their own. As though my fingers know what to do, even when I'm at a loss. Can I trust their intentions? I reach out my hands to scratch her face, but then, without scratching her, I pull them back.

She remains still and looks at my curled fingers. How long will you stay? she whispers, you and your little brother? I don't know, I want to reply. Don't stay here too long, she hastily adds. Her eyes dart around uneasily and she whispers: Come over one day, and I'll tell you about Notpla.

She points to the house beyond the fields, near the church, and holds out a little cluster of red currants: Come visit! Have a taste. We're allowed to eat them. They turned ripe the morning you arrived.

Has she been watching us this whole time? I wonder.

Was she the one who followed me when I fled here through the forest?

She squeezes her eyes shut and grazes my face with one hand. Then she whispers: I'm telling you this to protect you. Last year, a boy and a girl disappeared while in Notpla's custody. She leans in close and rubs her cheek against mine. Her hair smells burnt. She's sweating. I'm afraid of getting infected, but the sensation of her sweet-smelling cheek against mine is the nicest thing I've ever felt. Here's some chocolate and nuts, she says and hands me a bag, and I ask whether the contents are uncontaminated?

She presses her forehead to mine. The smell of her skin reminds me of something I don't want to let go of. I have to keep her face close to mine to hold on to the sensation. I can't pull myself away. The small of my back is on fire. There's a stabbing pain in my stomach. The faint stench of cows from the field mingles with the scent of her skin.

Don't stay for too long, she says.

Suddenly she's several metres away. My cheek is cold now that she has torn herself loose. You're the ones who rescued him, not the other way around, she hisses, and the hissing takes a toll on her, making her cough. She clenches her fists. The veins on her neck swell. Her shirt clings to her body. Two large circles appear beneath her armpits.

She stares at me. Expectantly, as though waiting for me to say something, but I don't know what it is. If I knew, I would say anything right now to bring her close to me again. I smile at her, but I don't have the answer. Notpla yells at her to leave. She breaks away and walks off with faltering steps.

My hands are soft and warm. The rest of my body is clammy. I'm just a *child*. For so long I've thought I had to take care of someone, and so I assumed I was an adult. I'm a child. But am I the woman's child, or am I Notpla's? My hands are buzzing. Little Brother is sleeping. Notpla hunches over his computer's keyboard and shuts his eyes.

I stare into space through the gaping window. There's the woman again. Over by the dark tree trunk. I can't help but laugh, and the woman laughs too. Most people can't imagine what it's like before it happens, she says. I stand up. I'm ready, I say and notice that my vision has gone blurry.

Then we're silent. The woman gestures with her hand as though in farewell. Only now does she turn around and walk off down the road. She leaves me hastily, as though afraid of being followed. The morning's first sunlight strikes the asphalt and blinds me, making it impossible to follow her figure as it recedes into the distance.

Notpla turns on the TV behind me. An old football match. Voices cheering. Feet stomping in a stadium. Little Brother wakes up and watches too. The 1999 championships. The historic match this country won!

And while I listen to the football match, I think: I'm prepared to do whatever it takes, but I have no idea what that is. All I know is that if the woman asks me to follow her, I will. The wind takes hold of the pine branches outside. I wait for Notpla to fall asleep and then I cut off his birthmark. He yelps and strikes out at me. He screams and screams. I cover my ears. Do something, would you? he pleads. Save me! But I don't budge. Little Brother yells that I should get it over with. Afterwards, Notpla stares out into the darkness, pressing a cloth to his cheek. What's the matter with you two, he whimpers.

And I tell him it was for his own good, so people don't mistake him for the man in the church tower, the man they call the woman-killer. Notpla's cheek doesn't stop bleeding. I have an unpleasant taste in my mouth, as though the birthmark somehow came into contact with my tongue. The sensation is so strong I spit in the sink, but there's nothing to see. I recall the feeling of cutting into the big, fat birthmark. It makes me nauseous.

I caress Notpla's cheek. It's swollen and infected. His eyes are smaller than usual, beady and fearful. Scathingly he meets my gaze. The veins on my hand are blue and bulging. Notpla stands up and roams around silently in the house. I don't try to get him to admit whether he too has seen a man who looks like him up in the steeple, the man with a birthmark. I don't ask why he refuses to speak to me about the birthmark I cut off.

It's morning. Notpla is lying in a long coffin on the floor. I peer down at him. Little Brother is distressed. Slowly I realise that Notpla is alive. He has tied a thick, white rag around his neck, and the rag looks like a big tumour, or a second head protruding from his neck. Little Brother has got out a shovel.

We have no choice, he proclaims and marches outside. I watch his movements as he digs a hole in the garden. I don't attempt to wake Notpla. I realise that Little Brother looks like him. The hole he has dug for Notpla has become too deep for him to climb out of himself, so I go out and help pull him out, and we return inside. Little Brother kicks off his muddy boots in the hallway.

Notpla rises from his coffin, which is still on the sitting room floor. He looks bewildered. Well, now the coffin's ready in any case, he announces uncertainly, and brushes dust from his trousers before sliding the coffin into the corner with his foot.

The woman is back outside the window, looking in at me. I close my eyes for a moment. Then I open them and swing the window open. The woman closes her eyes, purses her lips and says: I haven't been infected! She laughs hysterically for a few seconds. Then she opens her eyes again and falls completely silent, backs away from the window and drops her head so her hair falls forward, covering her face. She lifts her head up and swings her hair back in place. Now her cheeks are red. Some people say hiding here is untenable in the long term, she says.

Sooner or later someone will come for you, she says. The heat outside has intensified.

Notpla is calling. Hastily I close the window.

Little Brother pours coffee into plastic cups, three purple cups, and sets them in front of us on the table. He's in a good mood and has cooked rice. He wants me to humour him. All at once I see how much he's changed, how he's grown.

What is it? asks Little Brother with a laugh. He takes Notpla's binoculars from the table and peers out at the church tower. The windows at the top are now closed. Restlessly, he sets the binoculars back down and turns on the TV. Again, the same football match from 1999. The same clip of the crowds cheering and stomping.

If it weren't for the tumour on my neck, chuckles Notpla

suddenly, I'd be in prison, don't you think? He goes on, but I can't hear him anymore, because Little Brother turns up the volume. The whooping voices grow louder, like roaring waves. Notpla stands up and brushes off his shoes. This heat is intolerable, he yells, stomping his feet on the doormat, and then walks out the door. It slams behind him.

There's the woman, on the sofa. With Little Brother. The whooping from the TV continues, and I can't see Notpla anywhere outside. What would he say to this woman having sat down in his living room? I wonder. I want to say something to the woman or to Little Brother, but I can't move my lips. All I can think of is where in the world Notpla could have gone.

The woman has turned her face away and is studying the intricate patterns on the floor. Little Brother is on her lap with his face turned towards me, but he seems to be looking straight through me. I look at him intently. Smile. Try to get him to smile back. The woman wraps her arms around him. His body has changed. His face has grown smooth and childlike. Little Brother has become little again.

Someone knocks at the door. Hard. Notpla shouts from the other side: Who locked the door!? The woman fixes her gaze on the TV. Beads of sweat drip from down her neck. I want her to stand up, to tear herself away from the football match and leave the living room. Little Brother has fallen asleep in her arms. As long as she's here, maybe all of us are at risk of infection. I can't move.

Notpla goes on pounding at the door and yelling. The door doesn't budge, and I don't say anything, don't open up. All of a sudden *I'm* the one sitting on the sofa with Little

Brother in my lap, with no idea how I got there. I feel dizzy. My vision starts to blur. My eye sockets are throbbing. I cradle Little Brother in my arms. He clings to me.

Where's the baby carrier, I think. The woman is gone. She could easily have slipped out of sight without me noticing. Now it's just me and Little Brother on the sofa. My little brother, my little boy, in my care.

The baby carrier is on the floor. I recognise that carrier, I've carried it many times, for hours and hours along roads and through forests. Once there was a pram to go with it, but I can't remember where it is. I'll have to take the back door, I think, if I'm going to have any chance of escaping before Notpla gets in. The back door is never locked.

My vision is now so blurry I can hardly see, but I'm keenly aware of my arms and legs. My lips hush the boy. I pick up the carrier and strap my little boy into it. Then I slip through the kitchen and out the back door, moving as though I were blind. I know the way across the fields towards the forest. The mud. The slanting rain. The moist air in my lungs. I fear that my baby will cry in his carrier and Notpla will hear us.

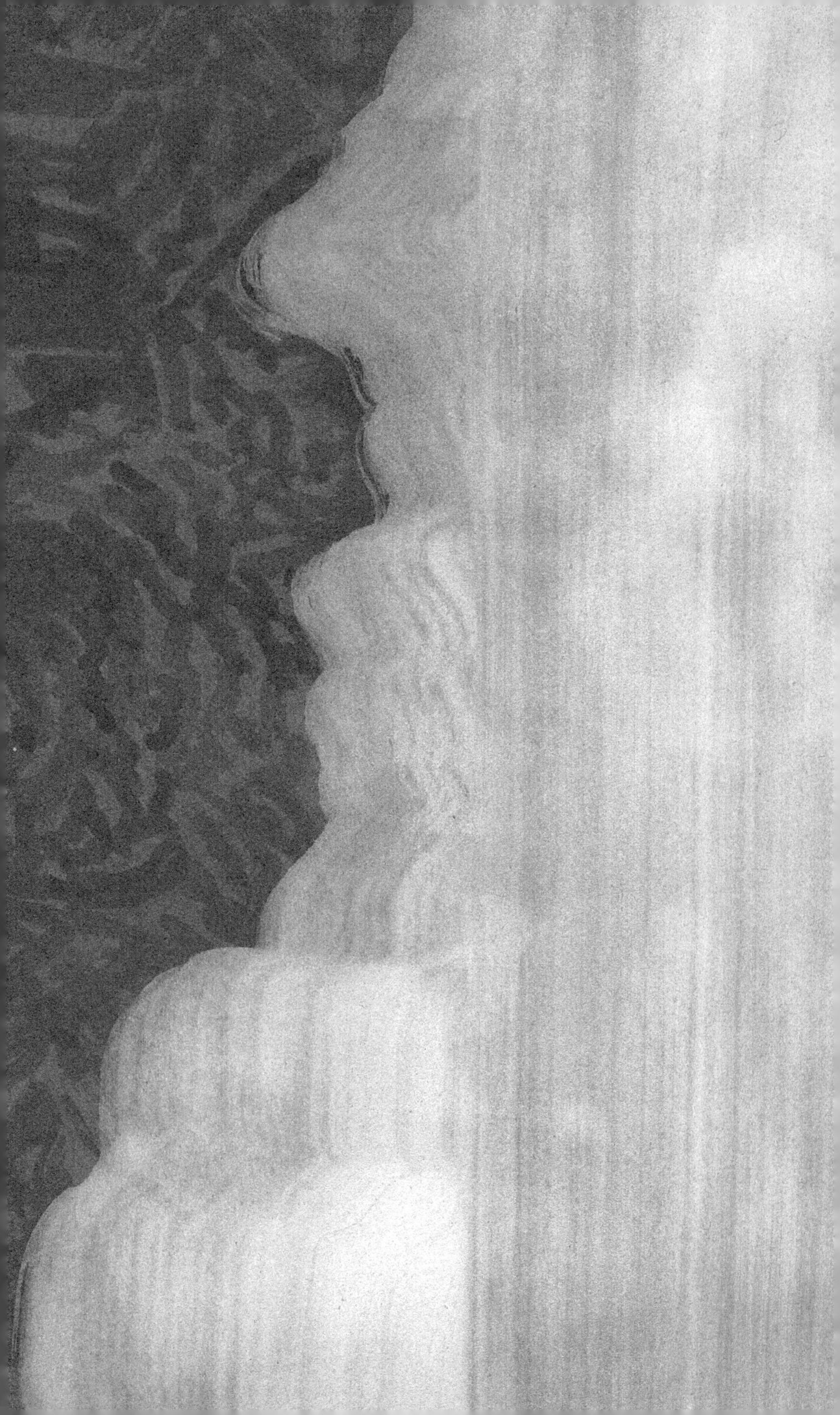

Compartment

It's been three days since our mother died. Her name was Nasfa, and that's all we've ever called her. There are three of us, in a compartment on a train making its way through Germany, to Hungary. On the floor between our seats is the narrow coffin in which Nasfa lies.

The train has called at Bad Iburg Station in the Teutoburg Forest.

I carve my brothers' names into the windowpane with the rusty pocketknife Nasfa once gave me: Miska and Jakub. They're asleep in their seats across from me. The station is made of red bricks. Many of the tracks are covered by big, gleaming puddles that ripple in the wind. The water trickles onwards, across the thistles and grass peeking up.

I want to get out of this train, Jakub wakes up and declares. No, please stay, I beg. We have to guard the coffin. Both of my brothers scratch their brown beards.

Our red train starts up again. It's night, but we can make out the dark green trees of the forest extending as far as the eye can see. At another platform, an old, brown train starts with a shriek, and water splashes up from the tracks across its rusty sides. Miska wakes up, too. There's no point, he mumbles. Let's get rid of the coffin! Bury Nasfa in the forest. Impossible, I whisper.

Nasfa is dead. I trace my brothers' carved names in the window with my nail: *Miska* and *Jakub*. The train is nearly empty. We're headed for Eastern Europe, to the home of our mother's ancestors. Our plan is to bury the coffin in Köbölkut, the village in Hungary where Nasfa's family came from. We've never known Russia nor Hungary, only heard about the deportations and wars.

When Nasfa told us about the deportations, we would reenact them afterwards. She would sigh and bury her face in her hands, and we would feel exiled, just like she had been. She had heard stories of Hungary every day when exiled in Russia, where she and her Hungarian parents, relatives and friends all felt like strangers. Later on, Nasfa and her parents had returned to Hungary, only to flee the country for good after the Russian invasion. Only Nasfa had survived the flight.

When Miska, Jakub and I were children, we would look out at the rosehip and dandelions in our garden, and even though we were free and had lived our entire lives in this house with the garden, we too felt trapped, estranged and exiled.

We don't belong here; we don't belong anywhere, Nasfa would often tell us. And we too felt as though we belonged nowhere. Sooner or later, we'll go home, Nasfa said.

Once, as I lay on a fallen tree in the wheat fields in the vast, silent landscape, I had tried to imagine my mother's relatives, under fire by the Russians during the deportation from their hometown long ago. Nasfa's family had been forced to bury several of their friends along the way, but the soldiers had ordered them onwards, threatening to shoot them if they didn't hurry up, and then shot at them anyway, even when they did pick up the pace.

Now Nasfa is lying in a coffin in our compartment. The train is headed for Hungary.

The train has stopped at Hannover station. There's a faint stench of rot from the stagnant water covering the tracks. All this stopping is driving me crazy, says Jakub. I can't take it anymore.

Those were the words Miska had said just before Nasfa passed away. In the end, her breath had been so raspy and she was so clearly suffering that Miska, after listening to her sickly breathing for a while, declared: I can't take it anymore. Then Nasfa let out her last breath, and he cried: Come back!

Miska and Jakub stare out of the window. The train has travelled a short distance only to come to a halt yet again. The darkness makes it hard to see what's going on outside, but we hear the screech of wheels and voices shouting in German. The hum of a machine that probably sucks up water, and a chemical fume, which is spreading.

I brush my hair. Miska and Jakub don't understand why I want to keep myself from deteriorating. The train starts up again. Every so often I'll think it has started to snow outside, but it's only the sparks from the glimmering tracks. We boarded this old train together all the way back in Hamburg. Some of the compartments are big enough to fit a coffin.

One of my brothers cracks his fingers beneath the blanket. The train stops at Magdeburg station. The platform is deserted. Only thistles and tall grass between the rails, and next to us, a high-speed train that looks new but can't continue due to the water covering the tracks.

When we first set out on our journey, Nasfa was in this compartment, travelling with us to Hungary, the country where her parents were born and later deported from. Then the train stopped for two days, and she got sick and died.

The floor of our compartment is still wet after a flood in central Europe. I tell stories about Nasfa with my feet on the towels we've laid out. Once a day I go to the toilet to empty myself. I vomit, too. We eat fermented foods from jars. Childhood rushes by like a breeze. They're asleep, my brothers. We're approaching Leipzig. I put up my hair with one of Nasfa's hair clips.

The train starts to move again. It's about time. I can't let myself sleep, because it's my duty to keep watch over my brothers. I wash myself so I won't smell. The air in our compartment tastes of iron, of old blood. The handles, the seats, the window. When we open the window, the stench of putrid water gets in from outside.

We've reached Leipzig. The station is enclosed in a dome of glass. *Jakub, Miska,* it's Anna, your sister! Can you hear me in your sleep? Your fingers are getting so thin.

The train travels a short distance, then stops again. No one boards or alights. People wait with blankets draped around their shoulders, perhaps unable to continue their journeys. Through the window, we hear over the loudspeaker that several departures have been cancelled. The platforms are wet. Black puddles remain in some places. In the dark, which is only partially lit up by tall lamp posts, it's hard to tell whether it's water or oil.

I turn away from the window and look around: Our compartment has black walls, black lamps of chrome. The threadbare curtains still have a bluish tinge to them. The folding wooden tables are brown. Even the windowpane seems quiet here. The seats are weighty and calm, reticent and waiting.

I think they're listening; Miska and Jakub. I tell them: If you think about it, Nasfa was in exile her entire life. The train screeches and sets into motion. Its heaving rhythm starts as a rumble beneath our feet.

Death is preferable to fascism, Nasfa often said. Each year, on the night of September 25th, Nasfa would hear a knock at the door. It must be visitors from Hungary, she'd exclaim.

The 25th is the commemoration day introduced recently, and much too late, to honour the deported Hungarians. Nasfa always hoped for visitors that day, but no one ever came.

We belong together, the four of us! Anna, Miska and Jakub and Nasfa. The train stops. The station in Dresden is also topped by an enormous glass dome, held aloft by arched columns.

Nasfa's parents stored jars of fermented food in case they were ever forced to hide in the bunkers. Her mother had been preparing the fermented vegetables while she watched the Nazis invade their Hungarian village through the window. Later, when the Russians marched and raped their way through the streets, Nasfa's mother had been making jam. Those in exile didn't remember the Russians as liberators, they remembered them as ruthless animals. Russia was surely hell on earth.

The train is moving now.

We'll get there eventually, I say. My brothers don't hear me, they're leaned against each other, dozing. I don't mind, I'm used to it. They've slept almost the entire time since Nasfa died. There's just a single pane of glass separating us and the clattering signs, clocks and blackened boards of the platform that glide past outside. The platform is dimly lit by torches. There must have been a power cut.

My brothers slumber on. Nasfa used to fear the day they'd grow up and turn into the men they've now become. She would sit by the window in her curry-coloured coat looking at pictures of Miska and Jakub as little boys.

Wrapping her coat more tightly around her, Nasfa had hissed: Men only think of power and acceptance. Her laugh was like a snowbell. Death is preferable to Nazism, she muttered grimly.

I don't want to lose my mind. I forget so easily, I whisper into the compartment and draw my legs beneath me, because there isn't room on the floor. The coffin takes up all the space in the middle of the compartment. In his sleep Miska stretches out his legs and rests them on top of the coffin.

My brothers ought to tame their beards and finish their food! They both have dirty plates on the little brown tables they've left unfolded. Let's talk, I tell them. We have more long-life milk in the bag. I try to take care of them, but Miska kicks off his boots in his sleep. One lands on the lid of the coffin with a thud, the other falls to the floor. His socks are full of holes, his toes are bluish, and there's nothing I can do about it. I fear that it isn't just the cold, but a nascent disease caused by the rotting water on the compartment floor.

Soon we'll bury Nasfa in Hungary, I loudly announce. Jakub complains of a headache. I've put on lipstick today, after forgetting the past few days. Nasfa always wore lipstick, no matter what. Dark red. Miska and Jakub are slumped against one another.

Childhood rushes by like a breeze: I see the thickets, the beech trees in the garden, and I recall the scent of apples, rosehip and dandelions. We were almost always outside playing in the tall grass, and when we came back inside the house, Nasfa would be staring out into the dusk and say: We Hungarians are always deported, our souls are always raped.

We did not understand the stories of her childhood in exile.

Our garden consisted of goutweed and dandelions, rosehip and old fruit trees, and it was full of weeds, which Nasfa insisted we let be. She said: We Hungarians are always purged, persecuted, denied our rights. Yanked up by the roots.

Now she's in the coffin.

The train has stopped next to a pasture. Miska wakes up and looks around in bewilderment, and for the first time on our trip I don't know where we are. There are no signs. Outside, the light is low. Miska peers out: Why have we stood still for so long?

Jakub is resting his feet on the coffin as if it were a footstool. It seems as though the train will never continue. I'm hungry and impatient for the train to start running, and I'm certain I smell petrol from the can beneath the seat.

It's time you hear the truth, Jakub mumbles, but then he falls back asleep without another word.

Is it malicious of me to go on talking about Nasfa? The window is shut. It really does smell of petrol. Childhood rushes by like a breeze. My brothers blink their narrow eyes. Their hair is brown. I slip my hand into my right pocket and touch Nasfa's medal. I sit quietly with my hand in my pocket, clasping the medal.

Listen, I tell them. Don't go to sleep yet.

But they've already fallen asleep. We're moving. The train rumbles along. It's as though my brothers can no longer keep themselves awake for more than a few minutes at a time.

Remember when the train stopped for two days, and Nasfa sat upright in her seat the entire time, right until her death? I ask. Jakub's lips are dark. Somewhere we are overheard and someone sets off in our direction, I think to myself.

Why do my brothers open their eyes so briefly only to close them again? Has the new year already begun? We're a family travelling through Germany to Hungary. All I ask is that we arrive.

Nasfa knew all about the wars between the Russians, Germans, Hungarians. Who won and who believed that they won. Death is preferable to communism, she said.

While in exile, all the deported Hungarians, including her parents, would hide in cellars when the Russians came to Russify them. Nasfa did not fear the Russian soldiers who wanted to teach the exiled Hungarians to forget their country, to lie about their past and unlearn their mother tongue. Instead, she ran outside and sang Hungarian songs.

Remember, Miska, Jakub. I will continue to remind you. Nasfa did not fear the superior forces!

Let me tell you how Nasfa became a hero. She was only a child when she broke out of her parents' cellar, strolled down the detested, dusty road in the exile town and spoke to the Russians who patrolled the streets. After that, people knew that she was the only one with the guts to tell the Russians about the little vegetable patch her parents once had in their garden, about the bunker and the jam and the church in their hometown in Hungary, which she could picture so vividly in her mind's eye each morning, because she had heard stories of it since her earliest childhood. Nasfa berated those who had grown too comfortable in exile, and to the soldiers, she yelled: I curse Russia, and she accepted the beatings that came after.

Later, when we were children, she had refused to let the rebellion go. She would shout across the garden's rosehip and dandelions: We're leaving! We'll tear down Europe's barbed wire fences along the way. We'll build a new city! We're headed for better places. The only question is where. To Turkey? India? Canada?

Jakub shakes his head and closes his eyes.

Miska and Jakub wake up simultaneously: Good morning, Anna! Won't you come outside with us? asks Jakub. Up into the mountains! Follow the hungry birds. We won't be bothered by the water up there. We've got to forget Nasfa! Find some people... Look, there's smoke from a bonfire...

I bathe in their gazes. My brothers are truly awake, the both of them, with their eyes on me. Each night I think about going out and burying her some arbitrary place in Germany, Jakub continues. Giving up. We'll never make it all the way to Hungary on this train, he says.

I look down at the compartment's still damp floor.

Remember, our mother was a hero to the Hungarians exiled in Russia, I rave euphorically.

But right now we're in a compartment. Deep within Eastern Germany. Us three siblings, I say… Jakub stands up. No, he retorts. No, you're wrong! Then, exhausted, he lets himself tumble back into his seat and falls asleep.

I can picture my brothers as two beautiful children. *Bartholdy Miska*, *Bartholdy Jakub*, boys in the thicket. In the garden, the scent of rosehip, always outside playing. Echoes when you shout in the forest. Reflections in the air. Summer days and Nasfa's depression.

As we slowly make our way to Eastern Europe, I hear the sound of the wind in the fruit trees of our childhood garden, I think of crisp autumns and the darkness above the fields.

We can't forget, I tell my brothers. Nasfa was an angel! How was it she walked? Bouncing. I stand up and bounce. Like this! She would clamber up the tree trunks when we went for walks and swing back and forth from big branches, I say. She would sing: I'm a human. If I die now, I'll go to hell. Death is preferable to nationalism.

We can't forget a single detail, I tell Miska and Jakub. We should all call each other Nasfa! Look, I still have her medal.

We're approaching the Czech border.

Jakub stands up again. No, he says. Stop it. You want to

know the truth? Nasfa was just another displaced person who didn't resist. When the Russians marched through the streets, she hid, just like everyone else, he says. Nasfa died of shame because she never resisted! That's what Jakub says.

I rummage in my pocket for the old photographs of Nasfa and us. Three heads of the same snake. Look at us! Her children, I say, handing him the photographs. Those pictures keep me alive. See the medal around her neck? It's impossible to overlook. That was the medal she was given during the exile because she alone dared sing Hungarian songs in front of the soldiers.

Quiet, please, says Miska, I want to ring Nasfa's phone. Just to hear her voice on the answering machine. Do you want to hear her, too? Miska asks. Jakub and I nod, and Jakub says: Why not? Miska looks at me, wais and sighs. But in the end he doesn't call, just closes his eyes.

Nasfa used to sit at the station café drinking tea at eight in the morning, I say. With her lips pressed tightly together, she would remember the gauntlet run into exile. The elders who were shot down, the children who died of cold and starvation. She could sit that way for hours, recalling their faces, until she could no longer stand it and left without finishing her tea.

She was the kind of person who might sometimes beat the Russian soldiers with sticks and shout out the names of those who had died during the deportation, I say.

Jakub shakes his head. She hid from the soldiers when they marched through the streets, just like everyone else, he says. That was why she survived and why she died of shame. Later on. In this compartment.

I ignore him and try to sleep.

Good morning. My brothers are asleep again. I've spent the past few hours bowed over the coffin. We're deteriorating, I say. We're travelling through the Czech Republic. The few people waiting on the platforms look right through the train when we pass them. They despise us, I think. Stay with me, I say, Miska, Jakub. I'll deteriorate if I don't speak.

The West falsifies history, Nasfa used to sing. She would walk through the streets singing: Death is preferable to capitalism. We lost sight of her. Now she's gone.

The train has stopped in Litomerice, the Czech Republic. It's become colder, and the three of us have bundled ourselves up in blankets. Here there's no rain and no flash floods. The station looks like a palace with its gilded lions and marble gates. In a thousand years, we'll be discovered as four rocks, four fossils, and we'll be alive inside those rocks. The world around us will have turned white. The darkness will have ceased. We'll always be together. Miska, Jakub, Nasfa and me.

The same words keep coming back to me: Nasfa is dead. She's in a coffin. We're on the train to Köbölkut.

My brothers are asleep. I've run out of sleeping pills.

The train starts again. I put on lipstick. Miska opens his eyes and looks around. The compartment doesn't move, but the train does. Jakub leans in close. She committed suicide out of shame, he says suddenly. She drank the petrol. That's what happened. There's nothing more to say. He squints his eyes. His beard has grown longer.

All those who deported us were men, Nasfa once told me over the phone. Russia, she yelled, where is that? It's dead.

America is dead. Scandinavia is dead. Man is dead. The only thing that exists is the power of women.

The beard on Jakub's chin makes me uneasy, even though I know that neither he nor Miska could ever harm anyone. Their beards simply grow, and they forget to trim them. The hair on their arms grows quickly.

Miska and Jakub sit across from me, always the two of them. I wish my much too skinny, emaciated brother, Jakub, with his pasty skin and his body always slumped across the seat, would break into a smile on his distinctive face, just once.

Today is a glorious day, with bright light and snow.

Brno station.

I'd like to go outside. Just for a moment. I smile at the few passersby on the platform, but they seem to look right through the train, noticing only each other. They're very tall, dressed in dark, elegant clothes, incessantly chattering. Then their figures vanish in the thick snow. I wrap myself in the beige wool scarf Nasfa gave me. It's just past seven. Miska is reading a comic book. Outside, the birds squawk and flap about before landing on signs and lampposts.

The sun is already setting behind the station now. We got several hours of bright sun today! These days, it's usually always dark outside. The train waits. The platform is well kept. The rubbish bins have gold fittings that gleam in the dim light. Two children in fur hats sit on a bench and stare straight ahead, seemingly oblivious to us inside the train.

Further off is the older part of the station. Here, the grass sticks up between the slabs. There are piles of bird droppings on the furthest benches and overflowing bins. A woman saunters past in high heels. A man with a newspaper under his arm and his black hat aslant walks beside her with his head turned away, talking into the air. Crowning the station is a small bronze dome, and at the very top, a blanket of snow. A silent plume of smoke escapes from a metal chimney. Dusk. Then complete darkness.

Four of us boarded the train together, Nasfa, Miska, Jakub and me, but only three of us will arrive. When Nasfa was still with us in the compartment, she whispered: I've wasted my time on men! Then she asked me to take care of the boys, Miska and Jakub. With tired, inscrutable eyes she watched her sons sleep and handed me the sleeping pills. We looked at each other. I closed my eyes for a moment and opened them again. She was still looking at me, clearly at a loss.

Later, her expression was simply closed. With resolve, she whispered: We've been at it for too long. Go to sleep. Here are more pills you can take when I'm gone, and soon you will grieve, just as I have grieved for most of my life.

I looked at her crumpled body, closed my hand around the pills and listened to her breath; I waited and waited, and she said: Now maybe I'll be able to sleep.

Miska looks around the compartment and then picks up the photo of Nasfa, Miska, Jakub and me from the table. The photo has been developed in black and white. He studies the picture for a long time and then slaps it back down on the table, hard. I think you ought to sleep now, he tells me. Staring out into the dark will make you sick. I tell him he looks the same as when he was little, and he strikes out at me limply and smiles. Your brown eyes look the same as when you were five, I laugh. It was your eyes Nasfa wanted the least to leave behind in the world. Miska doesn't reply. I turn away so as not to hear him snore tonight. He always snores. I put on my wool jumper over my dress. Pull the collar up to my ears.

Nasfa said: The disasters that befall you are always different than the ones you imagine.

I'm in the compartment with Miska and Jakub. Jakub is wearing his coat and scarf, moaning. He clutches his stomach and says the train journey gives him a stomach ache. If you disregard his stomach, which is bloated, he looks like a little boy and an old man at the same time. A long evening and night lie ahead. The endless tracks. I cough. Miska stares at the coffin, his pupils are tiny and sharp.

It's a tragedy, he suddenly says.

My entire body grows uneasy and my throat hurts. A biting wind slips in from the corridor. Jakub puts out his cigarette. I've put up my hair and done my makeup.

Let's just go outside, Jakub urges and stands up. Stop it, Miska exclaims, grabbing hold of Jakub and forcing him to sit back down. There are people who have been expecting us for a long time. In Hungary! How will they recognise us? asks Jakub. Our mother was a child when she left the country, they've never seen her grown-up face.

Miska has closed his eyes and doesn't answer. Instead he whistles softly with lips that are chapped. No one says anything. The moon is now visible in the sky. Jakub turns to each of us and laughs nervously on Miska's behalf. It feels like spring.

The train ceaselessly pounds out the same, steady rhythm as we approach Bratislava. Miska stares with narrowed eyes at the treetops that appear in the distance. His eyes are even narrower than Nasfa's.

Jakub takes off his wet socks. Anna, you always look like a boy in the pictures from back then, he suddenly declares.

I don't respond and start to file my nails. The train is moving, but we are not. The three of us sit very still. I look at the coffin. An old coffin made of dark wood with a fluted lid, carved with butterflies, cherubs and vines. The only nice-looking coffin we managed to find while underway. Remember how one of Nasfa's eyelids turned blue? I ask. Jakub pounds his fist on the coffin and hisses: Shut up!

What if the police at the border between Slovakia and Hungary confiscate the coffin with Nasfa in it? asks Miska. Don't you think we ought to set it on fire instead? Right now? The compartment already smells of petrol.

Miska is right, the smell of petrol stings in my nostrils. Jakub looks out of the window without answering. With an abrupt movement, Miska pulls something out of his pocket.

I have a needle from Mother's sewing kit, he says, showing us the old needle. Look, it's dull. It was the only needle left, and Nasfa asked me to take care of it. Take this needle with you to Hungary, she told me, and put it in the sewing kit along with the other knick knacks I brought with me from my home.

Look how worn it is, Miska notes, examining the needle

under the lamp. It's not sharp at all anymore, he says. And it's rusty.

Why don't we put the needle in the coffin instead? Jakub sounds defeated as he says it. Then he gives Miska a shove so he drops the needle.

The train halts with a shriek. Sirens can be heard from somewhere beyond the platform. The needle has disappeared beneath the seat. Miska lashes out at Jakub. You don't believe in anything! I've had enough. A needle, Jakub laughs. A needle as a replacement for Nasfa?! You're the one who's gone mad from this train. Stop searching for that needle.

I lean in and tell them to go to sleep. They cover their ears with their hands and turn away.

Everything has gone quiet, but only briefly. Soon the wind starts to pick up. A gust sends newspapers and tin cans scraping across the platform. Here at the border between the Czech Republic and Slovakia, there is neither snow nor rain. Outside by the station a horse passes a carousel that has stopped spinning. A couple of men are setting up a travelling fairground. Jakub watches them as they work.

We can't go outside anymore. We have to guard Nasfa, I say. I'm tired of staring at the carrousel. It won't be long before we cross the border to Hungary.

It's no use, says Jakub and gets up. Let's dump the coffin and go back to Germany. The Hungarian police will probably drag Mother out of the coffin anyway, Jakub complains. If I were any more sensible I'd hang myself!

If only Nasfa were here with us right now, Miska whispers. She was radiant.

Shhh, I whisper. Parts of Germany are already flooded. We can't go back.

My youngest brother Miska's clothes are now baggy. At this moment, his face is like Nasfa's. They look more alike than usual; his face has become even narrower and his skin is darker than before. But it's not just the two of them who look similar. In the photographs, it's apparent that all four of us have similarities, but we only resemble Nasfa, as if we have only a mother, no father.

Let me tell you about Nasfa, yells Jakub and stands up. Nasfa wanted to get away! She wanted to sit down with her back to the world and paint. She drank petrol to kill herself.

I thank Jakub and ask him to calm down. The train stands still. The seats have springs. Someone is singing in the next compartment. Miska mumbles and goes on staring out of the window. The compartment is cold.

Someone in metal boots paces back and forth in the corridor. Jakub yells: Nasfa put up with the taste of petrol and went on drinking until she had drunk the entire can. That's what happened! And then she went mad. That's how it is. That's how it goes. She drank petrol and went mad. She said: Just give up! The shame over wanting to survive in exile and hiding from the soldiers did it off with her, says Jakub. Shame catches up with you eventually, she whispered to me, and she was no exception. She doesn't want us to remember her story. What she wants is for everything to be forgotten.

Jakub collapses. I give him a piece of cheese. Jakub shakes me: Anna, listen to me.

We're still here, her three children, but we're the ones being forgotten.

Jakub pretends to be dead. His body is splayed out across the seat, eyes closed, leg twitching. Men in boots march past in the corridor. A door is blown open. Early morning? Night? We're the forgotten ones, Jakub repeats. But soon things will get even worse.

Nasfa was evil, says Jakub, looking straight at me. So I don't think I can do this anymore. Shoot me, Anna. Shoot me, Miska. I can see a red spot in the white of his left eye. He looks very tired. Everything that once caused Nasfa to flee, he yells, that's happening in Hungary all over again. They're shutting out foreigners. Let's open the coffin.

It's too late to open it, Jakub, says Miska.

The lid is screwed on, I say.

We stop at a town right before the Hungarian border. Snowflakes dust the quiet, empty landscape. Over the loudspeaker, an announcement is made in Czech. The train stands still for a long time. This time it's probably the snow preventing the train from reaching the border. It's no use anymore, Jakub screams. I want out. Jakub jumps up and glares at us with wild eyes, then he runs out of the compartment.

Miska hasn't budged for several minutes. He pulls something out from underneath his seat. The petrol can. Jakub is outside on the platform staring in at us. At first we were four, then three. Now there are two of us. The coffin *must* reach Hungary. On the platform, Jakub holds his hand to his mouth and coughs. He looks like he's freezing out there in the snow, wearing only his short coat. We have to stay inside. There's a rattle from the train's undercarriage. We watch Jakub stalk off across the snowy platform in a sullen farewell. Miska's legs are trembling. I scratch my scalp, and my fingers become bloody. Miska lifts the petrol can with two hands and sets it down beside the coffin. Jakub has laid down on the platform. Now he stands back up and runs around like a ghost, snow in his hair and on his coat. Doesn't wave. So he thinks Nasfa took her own life. That that was what happened.

A tree topples onto the platform. Jakub races off into the forest.

Now there are just the two of us, Miska says. You and me, Anna. The train starts. I think of Nasfa going swimming in freezing temperatures, just to feel the sea. On the train, she had told us: I'll die in this seat. She was sick. Now there are only two of us.

Miska has slept all night. We've been stopped at a new platform for hours. There are no signs here. Just a tall cliff-side and ivy. Thicket and fog. A lush, green landscape. Are Miska's toes frostbitten? I tuck Nasfa's wool blanket around his feet. The train starts to move. The names of Hungarian towns flicker by: *Gyór*. Mint-green houses. Birch trees. *Tatabánya*. Palatial yellow buildings. Tall green fences and green telephone poles.

Outside on the platform is a dilapidated sign, half-buried in snow so only a few of its letters peek out. ...Ö... Ú... Maybe we're here, I tell Miska. Maybe we've reached Köbölkút. He closes his eyes.

The snow has stopped. The station is small. Just a single line of tracks glitters in the lamplight. I stand up. It's practically pitch-black outside. Miska tries to get up too, but something seems to hold him down, and he shakes his head.

He hands me the matches and looks at me for a moment with narrowed eyes. Then he unscrews the lid of the petrol can and empties it onto the coffin. I can't move. He takes the matchbox from my hand, pulls out a match and strikes it.

There are two of us in the compartment. We're the same people as before, and the compartment is the same. But we alter the story around us. We're our own funeral; two heads of the same snake.